I0718836

Sally

L. MOONE

Copyright © 2020 L. Moone,

Cover art by eXplicitTales

Published by eXplicitTales

All rights reserved.

ISBN-13: 9781913930066

CONTENTS

***

CHAPTER ONE

Working for one's fuck-buddy is a funny situation to be in. One moment you're trying to be professional, then, you see them, or as in this case, get a suggestive message from them, and all propriety goes out the window.

Today is no different, judging from the words that have just popped up on my phone, while I was supposed to be working on a spreadsheet of sales stats.

'Tedious management meeting. Can't stop thinking about the other night… M'

Neither can I. Mark, who has got to be the sexiest man I've ever hooked up with, ordered some takeout for the both of us, allowing us to enjoy a not so quiet night in without the added hassle of cooking, or heading out for food. We tried watching a movie, but were quickly distracted by each other's company.

It's impossible for me to be near him without my hormones going haywire, and the feeling is mutual.

By the time the end credits rolled along, he had me bent over the edge of his bed and given me an orgasm I'll remember for the rest of my life. We finished the evening in the bath, letting the hot water calm our taxed muscles, while still unwilling to keep our hands off each other. All in all, a perfect night in. I went home before things got awkward for either him or me.

I respond with 'Likewise, perhaps we can do it again sometime ;)', and put my phone away before anyone comments.

My affair with Mark is common knowledge in the office, but luckily I haven't had to deal with jealousy as such. If anything, a few of them seem to feel sorry for me, or so they say, for getting involved with a guy who's never had a steady relationship in all of the five years he's worked here.

They don't realise that it's perfect how things between us are. I don't do steady relationships either.

★★★

"Is Sally Irving in?" This simple question, spoken by a familiar voice, rudely drags me out of my daydream and back into reality. *It can't be!*

Despite the years that have passed since I last heard this voice, and the fantasy I had just been absorbed in, there's no way I would make a mistake identifying this ghost from my past.

"You're looking for Sally?" I can hear Cath's clear soprano respond. As Mark's assistant, she's the one who usually deals with the occasional visitor to our floor. "How exactly did you get in here?"

I peek over my PC screen across the office towards the man with the bunch of tulips in his hand. He has his back turned towards me, not giving me much to go by, except the long-ish dark brown hair, broad shoulders, and faded brown leather jacket. Fuck.

Fuck, fuck, fuck, FUCK!

"Psst, Becks," I whisper shout, but Becky next to me, is so focused on her computer screen that she's completely oblivious to the disaster that's about to unfurl around me. The furrow in her brow tells me she's probably struggling with Excel again, which means she might as well have blinders on. She finally looks up when I throw a paper clip at her.

"What? Can't you see I'm in the middle of-" The irritation sounds through in her voice. I know she hates interruptions, but this is an emergency, damnit!

"Shh!" I slink back into my chair and gesture at her to keep her volume down. "There. That guy Cath's talking to. Please be a dear and get rid of him. Tell him I'm off sick or whatever. Or dead. Tell him I died last month. Try to make it convincing." My heart is hammering in my throat, making it hard to keep my voice from cracking and I'm starting to feel faint like all the blood has drained out of my head.

Becky takes a moment, scrutinising my face, before checking out the figure in brown leather. *Please, don't argue!*

"Fine. I'll do it, but only because I love you. Don't think you can get out of this without providing some sort of explanation later!"

I put my head in my hands and shrug. "Whatever. Just please, make him leave."

I hear her roll her chair back, followed by the click-clock of her heels against the shiny office floor.

"Cath, I'll take care of this, thanks." Becky's voice sounds suspiciously upbeat as usual when she's *handling* someone.

"So, who are you?" She asks the man. I half hope

he's just some random person who shares some familiarities with who I'm thinking of. Maybe a courier, who happens to have a voice that sounds just like-

"Gareth Doyle. Sally and I go way back." Fuck. It *is* him. Gareth. Now there's a name I've tried so hard and nearly succeeded to banish from my memory. Gareth fucking Doyle.

"Right, Mr. Doyle." Knowing Becks, and hearing the ridiculous tone she's using to address him, I have to assume she's enjoying this role a bit too much. Fine, as long as she does the needful. "Well it's terrible timing, Sally's actually on holiday at the moment."

"Oh. When will she return?"

"Not for a couple of weeks I'm afraid."

I lean up just enough to catch another glimpse, ignoring the risk of him turning around at some point and spotting me. At least from behind it seems he hasn't changed too much, even the hair is almost the same as I remember.

"Oh well, not sure they will last that long, but perhaps you can tell her I came by and left these for her." Gareth hands Becky the colourful bouquet.

"I'll let her know. Thanks." She keeps standing there, flowers in one hand, her other on her hip, waiting for him to make a move.

I breathe a sigh of relief, when after a few seconds of indecision, Gareth does indeed walk out the door. My hands are shaking, beads of sweat collecting around my hairline. *What the fuck was he doing here?*

And why am I so affected by him, despite everything

that's happened? It's totally ridiculous, bizarre even. I'm panting, as if the atmosphere has thinned out and I simply can't get the oxygen I need. *Jesus.*

Becky returns to our desks, and I can't face her. All I want to do is curl up into a ball and vanish. My stomach is all twisted up, confused and achy. If I'm not careful, I'm going to be ill right here.

"So. These are for you." She drops the flowers on top of my IN tray and sits down.

"Hey… Hey, Sal, are you OK?"

I once again cover my face with my hands, unable to wrap my head around what just happened.

"You didn't tell him I was dead. He's going to come back. I need to-" I can't finish; my throat feels dry, and I'm no longer sure what I was going to say anyway.

"What's wrong? You eat guys like that for breakfast, what's with this one?" Becky puts her hand on my shoulder, but I shake it off.

"I can't. Gimme a second." I get up and rush off towards the exit. *God, please make it so he's not lurking out in the hallway. Make it so I don't get caught!*

Luckily, the coast seems clear and I make a dash for the facilities. I need some alone time. No questions, no talk, just time.

The knot in my stomach is tighter than ever. Before I know it, I'm forced inside a stall, and faced with what's left of my lunch inside the bowl. Sadly, that doesn't do much to calm me down, just makes me angrier at myself. How dare he just drop right into my life while things are going exactly how I want them to? How fucking dare he?

My phone buzzes inside my pocket and I fish it out, with shaky fingers, managing to narrowly avoid dropping it into the mess in the toilet. It's Mark.

'Meeting just finished but you weren't at your desk. Let's go out, somewhere nice. French food maybe, or anything you like.'

Clutching the phone in my hands, I sink down to the floor, with my back against the stall door.

Taking a deep breath, I type out a typo-littered response. Sure, dinner would be nice. I guess. Ugh, I don't know anymore...

I was happy, dammit. Things were going pretty well with Mark, who seems to understand me in a way most guys don't. And now, all I see are complications.

I hate complications. That's the main reason I don't date, never have, ever since...

Why, of all times, does Gareth have to turn up now? It's been eight years, and only the latter half of them were worthwhile. After the hell he put me through, it took a whole four years to find my way back to normality again. Now, within seconds of seeing him, it's as if years of progress have been wiped away.

I thought I was over all this. I thought I was over him.

"Sal?" Becky's voice echoes against the tiled walls.

Shit, can't people get a hint? I decide to ignore her, but she knocks on my stall soon after.

"Sally, are you OK? Don't make me bust the door in."

"Yeah, I'm fine," I snap.

"Alright." Becky doesn't sound convinced, and predictably I don't hear her walk away either. "Then why are you sitting on the floor?"

Fuck, she's right. I take a deep breath, trying to focus my attention on the task at hand. Pass for normal, get the fuck out of here and think later. Or ideally, don't think at all, I've got dinner with Mark to survive without losing my shit.

"There, happy now? I got up," I say, after getting up and flushing away any evidence of my breakdown. If I'm going to make it to dinner, I'd better brush my teeth first.

"Sal? Who was that guy?"

"Didn't you hear him? His name's Gareth. Just some guy I used to know."

"It seems like there's a lot more to that story than what you're letting on."

"Whatever." I shake myself off, breathe deeply another few times to let my nerves settle, and open the door, attempting to act normal.

Once outside, I blank Becky and walk straight to the mirrors along the wall to fix my hair. Well at least I didn't cry. He didn't manage to break me completely. It's hard to look and feel halfway normal, with makeup smeared all over your cheeks.

"You know you can talk to me, right? You don't have to be some kind of lone crusader in all of this, it's OK to let people in sometimes." Becky is right, but I can't face her or anyone right now.

"Mark is taking me somewhere nice for dinner, I should probably finish off for the day and pack up my stuff."

Becky's reflection in the mirror shrugs and turns towards the door.

"If you change your mind, you know where to find me. Anyway, I have a date with Alex tonight too, so..." Her use of the word *date* grates at me. What Mark and I have planned is so not a date, and I intend to keep it that way.

When the door shuts behind her, I breathe a sigh of relief.

Her barging in here and insisting to check on me served its purpose as a distraction, but talking it out means releasing everything I've worked so hard to bury for years. I can't risk that.

CHAPTER TWO

As soon as five o'clock rolls along, I head out and across the street from the big shiny building that is Aspect Technologies and straight towards the little local supermarket for a toothbrush, followed by a quick smoke. Knowing Mark, he'll be a little late, giving me enough time to eliminate any evidence of my earlier meltdown.

Thankfully Becky didn't bring up Gareth anymore after I escaped her interrogation in the ladies' room, she was too busy making plans with her man, Alex. Those two are at the height of the icky in-love phase most couples seem to go through before things inevitably fall apart. It's both kind of cute as well as tiresome to observe.

As I head back in after finishing my cigarette, Becks passes me with a spring in her step uncharacteristic for the gloomy January season, which would see most sensible people brace themselves before heading outside. She, however, can't wait to get out into the cold.

"Later!" She flashes a wide grin, earlier questions clearly forgotten.

I give her a wave and head into the facilities once more. Time to transform myself as well as my mood, just in time for my non-date with Mark. One of the main pillars of my affair with Mark depends on keeping things light and airy. No suffocating emotions, no bullshit, no drama. It's imperative I leave my baggage behind.

After brushing my teeth, I redo my lipstick and add a few extra touches of eyeshadow and liner, just how I know Mark likes it. If he's still in the same mood as earlier today, I'll come around in no time as well. Hopefully.

No sooner am I done, does my phone alert me of a new message. Sure enough, just one word from him: 'Ready?'

I check the mirror one last time, seeing my reflection smile back at me through deep red lips. *There, that's better.* Just as I head out the door and across the hallway, he exits the office floor and greets me with an infectious, much more genuine smile than the one I had just practised.

"Oh, there you are." He obviously checks me out, making my skin tingle with anticipation. "Have you given any thought to where you'd like to go?"

I shrug, and lean in for a quick hug, enjoying the feel of his athletic body wrapping itself around me. It'll be at least a couple of hours before we enjoy more of those intimate pleasures, and I cannot wait.

"French sounds lovely." And in any case, I intend to focus more on him all evening than on the food. Nothing like the undivided attention of a catch like Mark to make you feel alive.

"Wow, this place is amazing," I remark, looking around at the tastefully decorated restaurant. Everything, down to the earthy palate and subdued lighting aims to create an intimate atmosphere. It succeeds, too.

"Yeah, Cath told me about it. It truly is a gem." Mark gives me an intense stare across the table and the hairs on the back of my neck stand up straightaway. In this light, his eyes stand out deep black against his symmetrical, flawless face. As far as men go, he is quite something. Gareth would have nothing on- *What the hell is wrong with me? Why am I still thinking about Gareth?*

"Something wrong?" Mark reaches over to take my hand, the gesture matching his suddenly softened features.

I shake my head, trying to rid myself of those stupid, lingering memories. *Get back on track, woman!*

"No, I'm sorry. I guess I'm just hungry and it's made me light-headed. Would you mind ordering for me?" I push my chair back and grab my purse for a quick trip to the ladies' room.

He nods in agreement and starts studying the menu. Halfway towards the facilities, I wonder if I should let him know I don't do snails, but figure it doesn't really matter either way. For a change I'm OK to go with the flow if it means I'll get a moment to collect myself.

I continue on and find myself staring at my own face in the bathroom mirror. It might be just the light, or my imagination, but I look like I've aged five years in the last few hours.

Chill, it's just in your head... After dabbing some water

on my cheeks and forehead, and practising a bit of deep breathing, I'm ready for the world again, or so I hope.

By the time I reach our table again, a bottle of red wine and two glasses have appeared, along with a basket of bread.

"Here, this ought to take care of the lightheadedness." He offers me a piece, pre-buttered, and I gladly take it.

"So what's the occasion for all this? Have something to celebrate?" I ask while nibbling on the bread.

He smiles and sits back.

"What makes you say that? Can't I take you somewhere nice just like that?"

"Just like that, huh. Not that I'm complaining, but our usual M.O. has been to just take each other, wherever." I wink at him and take a sip of wine. Lovely, perhaps now I can relax.

His smile turns into a grin, flashing his perfectly white teeth at me.

"There's still time."

Studying his face, with the high cheek bones and sharp jaw, and especially those lips that manage to distract with just the right amount of fullness... I'm reminded of that first time I noticed him.

I was out one cold October night at one of my regular hangouts, a nightclub where unusually I was not having much luck with the male of the species. Of course a few were biting, as they usually do. But they were either too drunk, too obnoxious, too creepy...

When I decided to give up and call it a night, Mark

was outside, waiting for a radio cab. He caught my eye immediately. It was like a scene from a sappy movie; the handsome hero, with his jacket collar pulled up, finding shelter from the incessant drizzle against the wall of the building. We shared a cigarette, and some small talk, when he asked where I was headed.

Sensing the changed dynamic of the evening, I suggested his place would suit me just fine. A pause and a meaningful gaze later, he answered with a smile.

When the cab arrived, he offered me dry passage, protected by his jacket. The ensuing night was long, sleepless, featuring much naked acrobatics and multiple orgasms. Unusually for me, I stayed until he gave me breakfast and his phone number in the morning. Both were very welcome indeed. Neither of us asked what any of it meant, it was understood.

There's a distinct difference between a date, and a prolonged hookup. A date holds certain promises, expectations, complications. A hookup simply happens; there's no pretence.

Although we've met up with each other off and on since then, I know he's been seeing other women, as I've been open to the odd flirtation with other guys. Though it's been a while since I actually went home with someone else, not that I'd ever admit it. After Mark, most guys I ended up flirting with never seemed quite interesting enough.

We've never openly talked about these things, which is probably for the best. Familiarity, contempt, and all that jazz.

"So I was thinking, Paris would be nice despite the February weather…" Mark's soothing voice makes me smile.

"Paris?" Wait, what is he talking about?

"Yeah. It does fit the theme."

"Theme?"

"For Valentine's, silly. You must be really hungry. I'll ask how much longer it'll take."

While Mark waves over the waiter, I wonder what the preceding conversation was all about. It's so unlike me to daydream much at all, especially not in the company of others.

Then I spy the envelope on the table. How did that get there?

"Five minutes, apparently." Mark turns to face me again, then slides the envelope over.

"I have it all figured out, you just need to turn up with your passport on the day."

Looking inside reveals a pair of etickets and a booking confirmation from a rather fancy sounding hotel.

"Wow, just like that, huh?" I'm as yet unsure how to respond. Would I like to spend a long weekend in Paris with Mark? Sure. Do I like the connotations of celebrating Valentine's Day there together? *Errr..*

I shoot him a tentative smile, hoping to understand where his head is at.

"What's made you so romantic all of a sudden?"

He shrugs, and sits back.

"Relax, I'm not proposing. It's only a trip. A bit of

fun." His eyes are glued to mine, and although he is sort of smiling, his lips are tense.

"Although, I would love for us to move forward together."

With that, everything about tonight changes. Everything about *us*, every assumption I had made about what our relationship entails, is altered. I hate it when this happens.

"You know how I feel about stuff like that." I remind him, struggling not to sound defensive.

"Look, I know you're not ready to settle down. And that's fine. It doesn't have to be *that* formal."

It sounds like he's also having a hard time maintaining his composure. I wish he'd never brought this up.

"You say that as if it's all me." My earlier dreaminess has vanished, what's I'm left with is the cold, hard reality. All isn't how it seemed.

"At least I'm trying." *Oh no, he didn't!*

Something inside me boils over and claws at every inch of my being to give him my full, uncensored opinion.

"Trying, my ass!" I exclaim under my breath. "Don't think I didn't notice the frilly panties in the laundry at your place. Or the fake nail that made its way onto the passenger foot well of your car!"

He looks away, and refuses to comment.

"I don't care if you're fucking other people, just as long as we're clear this isn't just a one-sided issue." I cross my arms and wait, but he just shakes his head and doesn't say a word.

When the waiter arrives with our food, all we can muster is a mumbled thanks, before resuming our silent stand-off.

Admittedly the food is lovely, but the evening has been thoroughly ruined, so we rush through it and skip dessert. Ever the gentleman, he does drop me home, but I don't ask him to stay and neither does he insist. We part ways with little more than a nod.

★★★

What a fucking day. The mess with Mark overshadowed today's earlier shock, but only while in his company. Now that I'm back home, all of it hits me in full force.

Gareth.

I hadn't allowed myself to think about him in years. What he did to me was inexcusable but it did make me into who I am today. For that, I suppose I should thank him: I'm stronger now.

The eighteen year old me, who was so certain she knew what love was, no longer exists. I was such an idiot back then. Today, I know it's just a fairytale. A convenient plot point that adds the saccharine sweetness to every other Disney movie. The original German fairy tales had it more figured out: love, as well as life, equals suffering.

Nobody lives happily ever after, to think otherwise is risky. It opens you up to a world of pain and disillusionment.

And Mark? Jesus, what a hypocrite. I thought he was

different. His carefree attitude towards relationships had been the topic of many an office discussion after Becks and I joined Aspect. When a few of our new colleagues tried to warn me, when all they succeeded at was to make me like him better.

Is that really how it's going to go from now on? Even when I'm sleeping with the biggest manwhore in town, my magic pussy manages to effortlessly turn him? Many women might crave such a talent. To me, it's a curse.

I would've gone with him to Paris, had he not made that final remark before everything went south. It would've been fun: see some of the sights, enjoy amazing food, wine, perhaps a spot of shopping. And at the end of the day - or even during - retreat to the hotel and do what we tend to do best. Give the other guests something to be envious about.

After hyping myself up all over again, it's going to be impossible to just go to sleep. I opt for a hot bath and a nightcap instead, just when my phone dings and a message from Becky turns up: 'Don't think you're off the hook for today.'

Oh God, she'll be insufferable in the morning.

CHAPTER THREE : MARK

When I caught a glimpse of the guy, Gareth, leaving the building, and then noticed the bunch of flowers on Sally's desk which Cath and some of the others were excitedly gossiping about, something in me snapped. For too long, I've been complacent, simply going along with whatever our relationship or lack thereof entailed. I didn't figure I could ever date traditionally anyway so it's been convenient that she hasn't made too many demands.

I knew she'd been seeing other people. Obviously she assumed I'd been doing the same. But for some reason I thought that she and I shared a certain magnetism that meant that we'd continue to circle around each other indefinitely. Now, I'm not so sure. That guy showing up at work for her threw me off balance.

She doesn't owe me an explanation, she's entitled her secrets as I am mine. I don't believe in full disclosure, especially in relationships. Some things are simply too private to be shared, to be opened up to judgement. But I couldn't stand by and watch while the best thing that's ever happened to me runs off into the sunset with some loser with 80s hair and bad tattoos.

I remember the first time we met so clearly. Like it happened only the other night, not months ago.

This girl I'd been seeing, Leila, and I had a big row that night. It was the type of thing you can't recover from. Rather than stay over at her place, as I'd done so many times before, I called myself a cab and got out of there as quickly as I could. I waited by the main landmark of the region, *Luminous*, a nightclub that had seen better days. Braving the drizzly October skies had seemed a lot more cosy than hanging around Leila's place, where hell threatened to freeze over.

Sally came out of the club, managing to look fresh and radiant despite the ungodly hour, and we got chatting. She was quite something. Her mannerisms were deliberate and confident, yet everything she did from lighting a cigarette to checking her phone had a certain elegance to it. She almost seemed feline. Beautiful, with a hint of danger. She looked like she belonged somewhere more metropolitan, like London or New York, not in our quaint little corner of the world.

Her athletic frame was protected by an expensive looking woollen coat with a furry collar, her gorgeous dangly earrings promised that whatever was hidden underneath would also be stylish and chosen with one goal in mind: to complement her natural beauty. Her choice in fashion has always been like the expert cut to an already flawless diamond. For the effortlessness of it all, I envied her and felt drawn to her at the same time.

Before I had the chance to consider whether flirting with her would be overly ungentlemanly considering the situation, she had already begun.

Of course I wanted her to come home with me. Of course I'd pay for the cab. Obviously, I'd make her breakfast, pleased to no end that she decided to stay the night. A few weeks later, naturally I'd offer her and her friend a job. Sally isn't the sort of girl you say no to.

She got under my skin and made me forget for a moment how complicated my life was and had been for the past couple of years. We clicked between the sheets as well as during those moments when we needed a little break. Only with Sally could you get into a passionate discussion about the plight of Indie musicians, mere seconds after flopping back on the pillow, out of breath with sweaty locks still stuck to our brows.

Today, when I saw that Gareth person, I forgot how I had sworn to myself I'd keep my relationships simple. I instantly knew couldn't let her get away. After casually asking Cath for a restaurant recommendation, I started to work on a rushed plan to try to show her I could be more than just a cock in a suit.

I should've known the Paris idea would backfire so spectacularly. She wouldn't have had a problem with it on any other date, but I had been an idiot planning a trip for Valentine's. In my hurry, I had thrown every possible cliché into the mix. You don't sway a girl like her with heart shaped balloons and cheesy greeting cards.

All I can hope for now is that that Gareth fellow gets the same response. But considering how distracted she was all evening, I'm not liking the odds.

Perhaps it's best to forget the whole idea. Bury the

possibilities I suddenly saw, despite myself. Perhaps it's time I let her go.

She'd found some panties in my laundry bin and a stick-on fingernail in the car. How careless.

Of course she doesn't trust me. I wouldn't trust me either. Best I start looking out for my own survival rather than chase silly dreams which aren't meant to be.

With that in mind, I log on to the chat room where I've spent so many sleepless nights over the years. I'm not sure what I'm after, support to cut her loose or encouragement to try again, but it may just be nice to find a sympathetic ear.

CHAPTER FOUR

"Sally and you are close, so what do *you* think the story is?" Cath asks.

"I dunno, she hasn't let on," Becky responds. "She doesn't exactly share stuff, you know."

Fuck, here we go.

Both have their backs turned towards me, but Elaine, who's so far just been listening in has spotted me and started shuffling uncomfortably from one foot to the next.

"Don't mind me, I'm just going to do some actual work," I remark and nod at them, just as the two busybodies turn with guilty expressions on their faces.

"I'm sorry, Sal. But you're being so mysterious that we can't help ourselves." Becky plops down next to me and repeatedly tries to push a lock of her stubborn hair behind her ear, to no avail.

"Whatever."

"He was hot though, that Gareth guy."

I shrug, trying to block my old memories of him. As disinterested as I am in those fragments of the past, I care even less to find out how hot or otherwise he is currently. Deep breaths. *Some asshole from forever ago cannot hurt me anymore!*

"Elaine seems to have a thing for tats. Kept using the phrase 'the hawtness' so often it almost became tiresome," Becky says, then pauses for a moment before patting me on my upper arm. "Anyway, screw that. Have you seen Mark around? He asked me to pull a report first thing this morning, and now he's nowhere to be found."

"No flipping clue." Who am I, his minder? "Why don't you ask Cath."

"Already did, but she hadn't seen him either," Becks responds.

I turn on my PC, and shuffle around the papers on my desk in an attempt to look busy, but Becky's eyes continue to burn into me.

"OK, Sal. I won't ask what's wrong because you'd rather choke on it than tell me, but you're not fooling anyone."

I sigh and rub my temples. Goddamn Becky and her habit of always saying exactly what comes to mind. Shame she doesn't know when to let things be.

"I'm glad you're not going to ask."

"Alright then."

She pulls her chair closer to her workstation and pretends to be productive for a few minutes as well, before coming back towards me.

"Hey, shall we make a plan to go out? Just the two of us, no boys? I promise not to bring up anything you don't want to talk about." Her eyes have lit up and it's hard not to get swept up in her sudden mood swing.

A smile forms on my lips too, despite myself. Perhaps a girls' night out is just what I need. It would certainly beat sitting at home, driving myself crazy wondering why Gareth is trying to get in touch all of a sudden. Becky and I will have a few rounds, chat for a bit, be silly like we used to be. If only she can stop being so nosy and just focus on having fun.

"OK, sure."

"Sally, my office?" says Mark, who turned up behind us out of nowhere. "Nice flowers."

"Right." I confidently push my chair back, hoping I at least come across somewhat normal. Wonder what he wants.

Becky's eyes meet mine when I get up, but she somehow manages to contain herself and her quick tongue. The last thing I need today is her smart-ass remarks making an awkward situation even worse.

"Yes?" I ask, unable to decide whether to enter his office fully, or if this is something that can be gotten over with quickly.

"Please close the door," Mark says, trying to sound casual. Still, my pulse starts racing immediately. I hope and pray that this isn't a follow-up from last night, because I'm dangerously close to losing it again.

Still, I do as he says and wait in front of his desk until he finishes scribbling something on a notepad. He gestures at me to sit down, which I do as well.

"I wanted to apologise. I was out of line yesterday." No shit.

"I'm sorry too. It's a tricky subject for me."

"Hopefully it won't affect us working together?" He looks me straight in the eye, and yet I can't tell what he's thinking. It freaks me out when people act so guarded.

"Not at all." I shift uncomfortably in my seat. "It

need not necessarily need to affect anything else either."

There's no change in his expression, no twitch or blink. He gives nothing away.

"Thanks, that's all then."

Stunned, it takes me a few seconds of staring at him writing more nonsense scribbles onto his notepad to realise I've been excused rather abruptly. *Well, fuck you too then.*

Back at my desk, I decide to inspect the bouquet Gareth left yesterday, which had already attracted Mark's attention earlier. It's in a vase, with water and all, probably thanks to Becky.

I would've binned it.

The mixed blooms are colourful, cheery, and very out of character for the Gareth I used to know. All those years ago, he would've been more likely to buy me some spiky body jewellery, rather than *girly flowers*. There's even an equally girly card attached. Knowing Becky, she's probably read it already… I might as well…

Dear Sally,
What I did was inexcusable. I am so sorry.
Please allow me this chance to explain. The past eight years have been rough, for you too I imagine, and I'll understand if you never want to see me again after this.
But I must try and do my bit to make amends.
Yours,
Gareth

Fuck.

Rough, eh? For the first few years, that would be the understatement of the century. Lately, things have of course perked up considerably, and it's hard to imagine putting all that at risk to give him a chance to explain fucking dumping me on what was meant to be the best day of our lives.

I ought to ignore him, avoid him, never speak to him again. Do to him what he did to me.

It's childish, I know it is. And it wouldn't be satisfying because the current scenario isn't nearly as emotionally loaded as how things were when he let me down. What the hell is wrong with him? To think that after abandoning me when I needed him the most, I'd just welcome him back with open arms to let him *explain why?*

He's got to be delusional.

It occurs to me that my current state of mind is a lot more productive than yesterday's shock. Maybe hearing him out wouldn't be so bad, if I can remain sufficiently angry throughout. Telling him where to shove his explanation might bring me closure.

I stuff the card back into the little envelope and hide it in my desk to prevent anyone else from accessing it too easily. Just when I close the desk drawer, Becky turns up with two cups: tea for her, coffee for me.

"Thought you could use this," she says, while putting it down on my desk.

"Cheers."

"How are things between you and *the hair?*" She puts extra emphasis on her favourite nickname for Mark, who indeed has the most perfect hair I've ever come across in the wild.

Goddamnit, here we go again. If being asked about Gareth was uncomfortable, an interrogation about Mark and I would be a close second. Especially since I can't figure out why he's made a complete U-turn since last night.

I can think of only one way to derail this conversation: relying on Becky's complete inability to contain her own happiness whenever prompted.

"Fine," I respond. "Say, how come you're just squeezing me for gossip lately. Why don't you tell me about your own love life for a change?"

Becky blushes slightly and stares down into her drink while taking a sip.

"Things are great."

"Uhuh."

Her eyes dart back and forth between me and the rest of our colleagues, who are far away enough that they couldn't possibly overhear. *That was easy.*

"Alex and I are planning to-I probably shouldn't tell you this." Becky tries to keep a straight face, but soon a coy smile breaks through anyway. *Score!*

"Don't be a tease. Spill."

"Well I told him I quite like the idea of doing it somewhere less private… Somewhere with more fresh air if you get my drift." She fidgets with a lock of her hair while speaking. The innocence of that gesture is hilariously out of whack with what she's just said.

"You want to go dogging?! That's insanely awesome.

Are you planning to get people to watch?" I can't suppress a grin myself. Former good girl Becky continues to surprise me; she truly has undergone an insane transformation these past few months. What's even more of a shock is Alex's willingness to accept the new her. Most men would baulk at some of her ideas.

"I dunno… But a change of scenery would be exciting."

I lean back, warming my hands on the hot cup.

"Sweet. I'm proud of you, Becks. Hope you don't mind me saying you were a bit dull earlier, when you were still together with Jeff."

"I know. That's all in the past now." She sniggers to herself and puts her mug down, with that same smile still playing on her lips.

"Good for you."

I'd never admit it to her in so many words, but at times I am glad for her how things turned out with Alex. Obviously I had plenty of reservations before, which I've been vocal about. The biggest problem I saw was that whole disaster that happened a few weeks ago after they had lunch with her Mum and he seemed to drop off the face of the earth for almost a week.

His reasons were solid, but the poor execution would have made it near impossible for me to forgive him, had I been in Becky's shoes. She's a better person than I am.

"So, how about tomorrow night? Just you and me?" Becky says.

"Are you sure you don't need to ask for *permission* first," I tease. "After all, your man might have different ideas."

"Don't be a cow."

"OK. It's a plan."

CHAPTER FIVE

Another day, another bouquet on my desk.

As I walk towards my spot, I note that the all too familiar gaggle of colleagues has already formed. I'm sure they'll know the circumstances of how the flowers ended up here already. In fact I'm sure people on other floors whom I've never met before know all about my stupid fucking flowers.

Becky is spinning back and forth on her chair, while talking to Cath and Elaine with a thoughtful, all-knowing look on her face. As I get nearer, she finally spots me and shoos them away before I can overhear.

"Morning," she chirps.

"Meh." I let my handbag drop to the floor beside my desk and eye the flowers.

A different florist than the others, and their colours are more coordinated. The last ones looked like Gareth tried his best and did something totally out of character. With these, however, it seems like he had expert help.

"I haven't read the card," Becky remarks.

"You'd better hope you haven't."

"Read it! Come on, you know you want to!"

Goddamnit. I might as well, just to shut her up.

The tiny little envelope matches the dark purple of some of the whatever-type-flowers. My name is written on top in a vaguely familiar, neat handwriting.

Sally,
I realise yesterday's apology was anything but. If you let me,
I'll do better this time. I prefer a life with you in it, on your
terms. Perhaps we can talk it over tonight?
Mark

I casually pop the card back into the envelope, and drop it into my handbag, before anyone else gets their grabby hands on it.

"So? Did the hot guy with the tats from yesterday not believe my story?" Becky asks.

"Gareth? No, these are from Mark."

She breathes in through her teeth and scrutinises my face.

"Cath had mentioned he's been acting weird. Do you think he's jealous?"

"I don't know what he is." I turn towards my PC, signalling that the conversation is over.

Indeed, I'm not sure what to make of this. Has Mark accepted my stance on relationships or is this just an opening to try again? I do wish we could get back to how things were earlier: uncomplicated, but extremely satisfying booty calls along with a seemingly endless supply of intelligent conversation. And laughs, lots of laughs. Men like that don't grow on trees and I really did enjoy his company, no matter what we ended up doing.

Whatever he's thinking though, I've already made plans with Becks tonight. If there's one thing I won't do over this, it's cancelling an existing commitment. No matter how many flowers end up on my desk.

Realising he probably expects some kind of reaction, I do a quick scan of the office, noting that the door to Mark's office is ajar, but there is no movement in sight. Cath is nowhere to be seen either. Perhaps there's a meeting going on.

So I get my phone out, to get this over with quick.

'Hey. Thanks for the lovely flowers. Tonight I'm going out with Becky already, how's tomorrow night for you? S.'

That'll do. I put my phone away without waiting for a response.

***

"OK, so where shall we go?" Becks looks up while putting her things away. Her wide grin betrays her excitement at tonight's plan.

"Hadn't thought about it. Somewhere nearby? I need a drink."

"Sure." She glances at her phone one last time before slipping it into her handbag as well. "You're not going to be texting with Alex all night, are you? You two have practically been attached by the hip."

Becky sticks out her tongue at me and pats her bag.

"You're just jealous. My phone stays in here, just in case."

As if.

We head downstairs and out the door, where Becks offers me her arm. Together we stroll off, braving the wintery elements, towards a rather promising looking neon sign some distance down the road. Any old pub will do for me tonight. And any old pub it turns out to be.

Beyond the rustic wooden doors and fogged up windows I can just about make out a few dim lights and some silhouettes of others with similar evening plans. This isn't a place you end up when you're after sophistication and fine dining. This is where you come to drink.

"So, red or white?" Becky asks, with the barman waiting impatiently for her instructions. As if he's busy, I snort internally at the thought.

"Whatever you like, we can share a bottle."

Becky turns to order, while I scan the room. An old fashioned looking pub, with heavy wooden furniture and the obligatory old guy in the corner who's staring out the window while sipping his Guinness. His tweed jacket is about the same greenish brown colour as the curtains and the carpet. Funny, how every pub seems to have at least one of these characters. Hell, at least the drinks are cheap.

"Let's sit by the window." Becks nods at a grouping of leather arm chairs somewhere halfway between the door and the fireplace.

"Sure."

We discard our soggy coats and rest our feet. Although a good few feet away, the fire manages to quickly warm us up while we start sipping the fruity red Becky had picked out. Though not quite of the same calibre as what Mark and I enjoyed at the French restaurant last night, it's still rather nice.

"So, Mum's been asking about you," Becky remarks and puts her glass on the round table between us.

"Oh yeah?" I'm afraid to push, considering the dark expression on her face.

"I often feel like she considers you more her daughter than me."

I can't withhold a snort.

"If she knew me, I mean really knew me, she would think otherwise."

"Yeah well, tell *her* that."

Becky puts one leg over the other and observes me for a moment, as if contemplating what to say next.

"She hates Alex."

"She hated Jeff too," I respond.

"Apparently now that he's out of the picture, he's an angel."

I lean over and pat her on her arm.

"So the solution is simple, tell her you've dumped Alex. She'll be singing his praises in no time, then you can have a joyful reconciliation and everyone will be happy."

"That's not funny."

It is precisely these issues that make me glad I don't have to deal with such nonsense. No attachments means no drama. Or at least that was the plan until everything went to shit a couple of days ago.

"You know I'm not the best person to advise you here. Your Mum is a peculiar character."

"That she is." Becky sighs, with a stubborn frown on her face. "Or Alex and I could run away together and not leave a forwarding address."

I give her a stare and she looks back at me, until we both start giggling.

"Tell you what, you should sign her up on some dating site for oldies. She just needs a good lay." I grin.

Our giggles turn into full-on laughter.

"Oh can you imagine? My Mum on a blind date with some stranger off *the world-wide-web. You know there are too many perverts on the world-wide-web.*" Becky's impression is pretty close, but I daren't tell her for fear of freaking her out. Her worst fear in life has got to be the idea of turning into her Mum.

"God forbid if his shoes and socks clash, she'll have that sour expression on her face like he pissed in her entree."

We pour another glass of wine each and sit back, quiet once more. I feel for her, nobody should have such a complicated relationship with a parent, and without a proper reason. Becky is too sensitive, always has been, and her mother too set in her ways to see how she affects her.

"Do tell me more about your dogging plans though," I try to steer the chat into more cheerful territory. "Is it like a plan plan, or are you still on the fence?"

Becky blinks a few times and focuses down on her glass of wine.

"I'm all for it, but I do have some concerns of how it would really work, you know?"

"What do you mean, you go somewhere and get it on, what's so hard in that?"

"Yeah, but what if we like get caught?"

"Isn't that the whole point?" I wink at her.

She starts giggling again and shrugs.

"Well it's anyway not going to happen until the weather warms up."

"Unless you get a car…"

"Mhm."

Around us, the pub is starting to fill up, though not by much. A couple more regulars have sat down next to lonely Guinness man, and a group of broad shouldered manly blokes are standing by the bar, commenting on the sports playing on the telly.

A glance at the clock tells me it's nearing dinner time, but I'm not in any mood to get up.

"Are you hungry, shall we just eat here?" I ask Becky, who simply nods, while rummaging around in her bag, no doubt checking for messages from Alex.

I am compelled to check mine too, and am strangely excited to see there's a response from Mark. Tomorrow night, his place. Becks is still busy, her frustrations from earlier about her Mum seemingly forgotten while furiously typing a lengthy message. He does seem to make her happy, that Alex, which is nice. Some people simply aren't cut out to be on their own, and Becky is one of them.

I decide to respond to Mark as well, and whether it's the wine or something else, something makes me wish that we can get things worked out somehow. I'd rather have him in my life than out of it. He makes things more interesting, more fun somehow. And it helps that he's absolutely gorgeous.

When we're both done, we study the specials on the chalkboard above the fireplace.

The offerings are a perfect reflection of the rest of the pub: not very sophisticated but they'll have to do. And anyway, it's been a while since I've had Shepherd's Pie. We order our food at the bar and sit back down with another bottle of wine.

"You know, I've never told you this, but I wasn't always like this," I say.

Becky looks up while zipping up her bag.

"I wasn't always so - cynical." I rest my head on my hand and take a deep breath. Perhaps it's time she knew.

"Oh yeah?"

"I was supposed to get married... It feels like a different life now, but there it is."

"Shit, I had no idea!"

"It didn't happen of course, but-"

"Gareth. He was the guy wasn't he?" Becky's eyes are about the size of saucers as she leans over and takes my hand. "That's why you were so upset when he came into work."

I nod. After half a bottle of wine, it's somehow easier to let go of some of those so closely guarded secrets. They still hurt though. I still have to fight the prickle of tears in my eyes thinking back to it all.

"I was 18, he was a couple of years older. Our parents knew but didn't approve of course, not that they could do much about it." That's as much detail as I'm willing to divulge. She knows I'm not in touch with my folks, this should be enough of an explanation why.

"What happened?"

"Honestly, I don't know. Everything was supposed to be simple, just the two of us, we didn't share the specifics with anyone. The day we were supposed to meet at the Registrar's office together, he never turned up and his phone was off too. Like he'd vanished."

Becky's face has fallen about as much as it could. For once, my chatty best friend has run out of questions.

"Fucking hell." She leans back in her armchair and shakes her head.

"Yep."

"What an absolute douchebag."

"Yep."

"And now he's come weaselling back looking to make amends? The nerve on that guy."

"I know."

For the rest of the evening, the topic of Gareth doesn't come up, instead we focus on other people's lives for some much needed gossip.

CHAPTER SIX

"I was worried you wouldn't want to come over," Mark evades my gaze, instead looking down at his hands, in a rare showing of weakness. It's completely out of character for him, and actually kind of endearing.

"Well it's only fair we figure this thing out." I observe him, as he starts to chop the onions and garlic, in preparation for the feast he's promised me. Apparently he's making some kind of seared duck breast in a red wine something, I wasn't quite listening and anyway I'm not that much of a foodie.

"Indeed. Well, I've done a lot of thinking lately."

"Oh?" I awkwardly smooth down my grey pinstripe shift dress and take a seat on the stool opposite him at the breakfast bar. I can't help but miss the good old days when things between us were so much simpler.

"It wouldn't be fair to lie to you in order to keep the peace. I really did mean it when I said I want to move forward together. As a couple."

I'm about to protest, but he raises his hand signalling he's not finished yet.

"I know. You prefer the status quo. But I can't help feeling that what we share deserves more than the odd shared meal followed by sex."

"Great sex," I mutter under my breath, omitting the caveat that great sex tends to get ruined by labels and responsibilities.

His eyes squint slightly, betraying his amusement at my remark, yet he moves on.

"The thing is…" He leans across the breakfast bar and takes my hand, running his thumb over my knuckles in a way that makes me a little weak and hence uncomfortable. Yet I daren't pull away. "I really care about you, Sally. And I respect your side in all of this…" His voice trails off and we're left in silence, staring at each other.

I don't have the energy for another argument, if he truly does respect my opinion, hopefully he will soon drop it.

"What if…" He squeezes my hand gently before continuing, his gaze averted for the moment. "It doesn't have to be so rigid, so restrictive. So monogamous?"

His eyes flicker up and there's a flutter of something odd in my stomach. I can't tell yet if I'm about to have another meltdown or I'm just affected by his touch, his scent in the air, the memories of what else we've used this work surface for in the past.

"I don't get it." My voice sounds hardly more than a croak. How is it that his presence makes me weak, even when I want to do nothing more than to blow up and make him shut up about the relationship crap already? I must be losing my mind.

"I mean, how about we take baby steps. How about an open relationship?" He seems so boyish, vulnerable. For a change, the great Mark Lloyd, with the perfect hair, flawless bod and impeccable dress sense is completely out of his element, because he's not the one in charge. Strangely I don't feel in charge either.

I'm not sure what to say, I'm sure this offer, this compromise, was hard for him to suggest. I can tell by the look on his face. He's not excited about the prospect of an open relationship, he's just hoping for something more than what we've had so far. Our dinner together the other night made it clear that what he actually hopes for is only a lick of paint away from a white picket fence.

But he did suggest it. And he's not been faithful to me either, despite how he was trying to play it.

That must mean the offer is actually on the table?

All day at work I've been wondering, going back and forth on what Mark possibly wanted to discuss tonight to make things work out. I just want things back where they were. I need to forget about all the unwelcome drama of this week, and the best way to achieve that would be it's a good hard session of what we tend to be good at together. Dirty, nasty, sticky sex which in no way, shape or form comes close to the term "lovemaking".

I force a smile, and squeeze his hand for a moment before letting go. This is way awkward.

"Would it be OK for me to think about this?"

"Sure, sure." He retreats again, and starts rubbing the meat with some salt and spices. His expression is guarded but at least it doesn't seem like this will be the start of another battle.

"I mean, so much has been going on lately, it wouldn't be fair to answer without thinking it through properly," I mumble and continue to observe him.

He wipes his brow and continues to focus on the task at hand. The food. It's all a tad domestic for my liking, even if it's not the first time he's cooked for me. And I'm not even counting the attempts that evolved into hungry sex before the ingredients had even made it into the pan.

I wonder if all of this has only come about because he is indeed jealous of whatever he imagines Gareth means to me, like what Becky suggested. If only he knew the whole story. But telling Becky last night had already felt like pulling teeth despite the wine we'd shared, and I'm not ready to let Mark in on it. Not now, not ever. It's all way too raw still.

"So what's for afters." I try to sound cheerful, but to my own ears the bittersweet undertones are still obvious in my voice.

"Mousse au chocolat." He focuses his attention downwards after answering, and turns on the stove.

I consider my next move, observing him as he organises the utensils he's going to need. Something's gotta give, I can't stand this glum atmosphere any longer.

"I hear that tastes much nicer when it comes with a side of nipple."

He stops mid-movement, the duck breast hovering about a foot over the pan on the fire, and gives me a sideways look.

"A side of nipple, eh. I'll have to remember that."

The sight of him, distracted from the recipe he'd

painstakingly followed earlier, makes me smile. *Please, please, let things be more normal now!* Let's forget about relationships, open or otherwise, let me just enjoy his company for as long as I'll still have it.

The look we share, which seems to last forever suggests an understanding. Little by little, his guard comes down and he checks me out more like how he used to, before things got complicated.

Finally, he does put the meat, skin down, into the pan. It sizzles violently and we're almost instantly surrounded by the appetising aroma of duck. I sigh deeply, noting his changed demeanour. Perhaps tonight won't be so bad after all.

He picks up a bottle of red from the counter, and grabs two glasses, putting them next to one another in front of me.

"I hope you like duck pink on the inside, because I'm not sure I have the patience to cook it for too long." Mark removes the cork with a swift movement of the corkscrew and pours until my glass is half full. I think I see yet another glimmer of the old Mark in front of me, and decide to test the waters.

"Patience has never been your strong suit when it comes to female company, or so I hear," I tease, accepting the wine he hands me.

"Is that so? What else have you heard?" After filling his glass too, he raises it, clinking it to mine. Definitely, there's a bit of a smile hidden in those dark, brooding eyes.

"It's only rumour, of course, but I heard you prefer it

when female guests arrive for dinner already prepared for what is to come later. With as few *barriers* as possible in the way, if you get my drift." I take a sip, feigning innocence, but I sense his eyes burning into me, seeking evidence that I've indeed arrived *prepared.*

The richer scents coming from the stove break his focus on me for a moment, prompting him to step around to flip the meat. But then, he's back with a vengeance.

"You seem to know me very well." He takes my hands into his and gives me an intense stare.

I shrug and continue to play coy.

"I like to think I know your type."

He moves in closer, running his fingers over the back of my hands, and up over my arms. With me still seated on the high stool, our height difference is practically gone. We have perfect access of one another, but I continue to hold back.

I catch a hint of his cologne, which previously had been disguised by the range of other scents in his kitchen. He does smell perfect as well, always does, even after we've worked up so much of a sweat that I feel filthy myself, he somehow manages to remain enticing.

He leans in, almost touching his lips against mine, but then pauses in that most infuriating way, as if to make me beg.

I won't.

I can't.

But I must do something.

"Something's burning," I say. My throat has gone

dry, making my voice sound hoarse.

"Food's fine." Mark doesn't bother to check the stove, he's that confident.

"Right." I blink a few times, trying to fight the urge to give in to him. It's frustrating how much I want him, even though we seem to exist on completely different planes of reality. Why isn't this enough for him?

He makes the first move, bridging that final fraction of an inch until our lips meet. My reaction is instant; eyes snap shut, even though I wish to see more of him. I'll get that chance shortly, I'm sure. For now, I focus on the sensation of our tongues, touching only slightly at first in a playful dance which is teetering on the edge of control.

I wrap my arms around him, exploring the outlines of his shoulder blades underneath the smart light grey shirt he wore to work today. Although I know what awaits me, for some reason I haven't get gotten bored. Mark couldn't be boring if he wanted to be.

His lips have worked their way down the side of my neck, and his hand reaches around to unzip the back of my dress just enough to give him access to my collarbone which had so far been hidden underneath the high neckline.

"I'm not hungry, let's skip dinner," I breathe, and try to direct his mouth back to my neck.

"Give me a minute, I'm confident you'll change your mind." His breath against my skin tickles and gives me goosebumps.

He pulls away, leaving me vulnerable and wanting.

After bridging the distance to the stove in long, rushed strides, he switches off the gas and covers the pan with a lid and returns equally quickly.

"Now, where were we?" He offers his hand, which I take gratefully before sliding off the bar stool.

"We were having dessert."

His strong, toned arms surround me and before I can do or say anything he lifts me up, bringing my mouth up to his level. I wrangle the bottom of my dress up over my hips, allowing me to wrap my legs around his waist for added stability.

He kisses me and things seem to fall into place again. This is how things are supposed to be between us. Less talk, less drama, more physical connection.

While still in the midst of that initial frenzy which overstimulates the senses when you finally reach that moment you've been longing for during days apart, he somehow still manages to navigate through his lounge and towards the sofa.

I fall back into the soft cushions, and rid myself of the top of the dress at least, letting the bodice fold over and fall down on my stomach. He leans down, and kneels over me, pulling the whole thing down over my hips and all the way off my legs. Sitting on the armrest, he takes first my left foot into his hand, unzipping my ankle boot and discarding it on the floor, followed by the right.

"Indeed, you are prepared," he remarks, running his finger down along the centre of my stomach, from between my exposed breasts, towards where my panties should have been.

Thank God for hold-ups, because pantyhose would have made this little stunt uncomfortable, if not unmanageable.

I shiver, as his fingertip brushes over the narrow triangle of neatly trimmed hair which crowns my folds. Mesmerised, the only change in his expression comes as he licks his lips in anticipation. I know what's about to happen and I cannot wait.

"Don't. Go. Anywhere," he whispers, and withdraws his fingers again. "And close your eyes."

He sure knows how to tease… Still, I obey and wait for an agonising few seconds, unable to make out what the noises in the background are meant to signify.

Then, with a gasp, I'm startled, as something so cold it might as well be frozen hits my flush skin. My eyes snap open, to find Mark, leaning over me with a serving spoon and a bowl, after depositing a generous mouthful of chocolate mousse right in the centre of my cleavage. He lowers the spoon again, painting a line straight down the middle of me, a treasure map of sorts.

As cold as the dessert felt initially, it warmed to my flesh quite quickly, making each movement of the icy spoon almost as intense as the last.

He stands back, admiring his artistry and puts down the bowl. *Come on, dive in, I cannot wait!*

Sure enough, he kneels beside me on the carpet and starting at the top, licks the chocolatey mess off my skin, making it a point to indeed add a bit of nipple action. I writhe into the cushions, impatient for him to finish with my stomach and move lower down.

Please, please don't be gentle with me after this!

I moan, closing my eyes again, and gather all my willpower not to grab a handful of his hair, directing him to where we both know he must end up eventually. If only he wasn't so damn good at this, at whatever he sets his mind to, I may not even have turned up tonight. And even if I had, I may have left after he brought up the relationship stuff again.

But it's hard to go without this, this sweet torture he's putting me through.

"Good girl," he whispers in my ear, leaving my skin painfully unkissed once more. "Open up."

I obey, opening my mouth to the velvety taste of chocolate. Rich, with a bitter hint coming through that's just enough not to make it overly sweet. Perfect.

After the first spoonful, I open my eyes again to find him naked. His sculpted, though slim body is an image of perfection to match everything else about him. I signal at him with my finger to come closer, which he does, and then to turn around…

He understands me perfectly, when I move onto my side, allowing him space to lie down in the opposite direction next to me. Spreading my legs, he reaches back for the spoon one last time, depositing a dollop of mousse right where it matters.

"Ow!" I cry out, startled by the cold, then am forced to repeat the same outcry when his hot tongue follows almost immediately.

I thrust my hips into his face, while diving into his

crotch myself, taking his solid length between my lips. The slight saltiness of him is rather pleasing to the palate, how it cuts through and complements the richness of the chocolate he'd fed me earlier.

Meanwhile his movements between my legs deepen, his tongue burrows into my folds as he laps up every last hint of chocolate from my wet pussy. I can't help myself, twitching and wriggling so much he has to hang on with both hands to prevent me from throwing us both off the sofa.

And yet somehow, I manage to focus on the task at hand, sucking him with all I've got, deeply, but letting go every so often to slow down and lick the head of his cock like how I know he likes it.

His reaction is quick, the tremor in his tongue instant when I run mine over the slit right at the top. He pulls away slightly, and moans into my swollen, excited lips, before dipping in again just enough to tease my clit, causing me to react similarly. We're both running on autopilot almost, doing what we know best, pushing, goading the other further, in a fevered competition towards the finish line.

"Enough," he grunts, releasing me.

I smile as he gets up, knowing that I've all but won, even if he's taken my favourite toy away for now.

He gestures at me to get up, then grabs me around my thighs and swiftly flips me over his shoulder. It continues to be a surprise me how strong he is. Before I know it he deposits me right-side-up on the bathmat in front of his shower.

I shiver at the slight chill in the air when he turns on the water, which takes a moment to get up to temperature. Then, he leads me inside and I'm surrounded by the soothing warm stream, as well as his arms which have me pinned in place against the tiled wall.

Behind me, he spreads my legs to allow him access, and releases me except for one firm hand on the back of my neck. Then he plunges into me, filling me with that sweet sensation I'd been craving for days. He continues to hold me steady, with his other hand on my hip, while pushing against and into me, repeatedly.

His impressive girth, stretching my aching pussy makes my knees weak. Or perhaps that's still due to my conflicting emotions. But it feels so good I wouldn't want him to stop or hold back.

I'm grateful for the wall in front of me, or the intensity of his thrusts would have me wobbling about on my feet. Instead though, I brace myself against it, keeping a strong footing and meet his strokes with the resistance necessary to make it count.

He speeds up, intensifies the grip on my neck, before releasing me only momentarily to hang on to my wet hair. I struggle against his grip, willing him to pull at my hair a bit harder. As he continues to fuck me hard against that wall, I can't tell if it's the hot water misting up the shower cabin, or our combined efforts. Possibly a bit of both.

"Go on, finish it," I cry, causing him to go into overdrive, hitting all the right spots to send me into a tailspin of sensations.

I'd been close before, on the sofa, thanks to the expert treatment of his tongue, but now, it's becoming unbearable. He lets go of my hip, wraps both arms around me again and kisses and bites into my neck and shoulder, making me moan even louder. Yet somehow, he manages to continue the same rhythm, until I find sweet release and my knees threaten to buckle from underneath me. He's all but carrying me, pushing into me a final time and groaning into the back of my neck, with his arms still locked around me like a safety harness.

When his loosened grip allows me to turn around, I take the shower head out of its holder, and use it to massage both our spent muscles until our breathing has stilled to a more normal level.

"You were right," I remark, while getting out of the cabin to pick up some towels.

"Mhhm?"

"I am indeed hungry now."

He grins at me and gladly accepts the towel.

"Told you so."

CHAPTER SEVEN

Once again, I'm home and confused. Although in the end Mark and I had a nice evening together, I couldn't shake the earlier awkwardness completely.

I like spending time with him. I think I might even like him as a person. But I don't like being forced into things.

Men have an awful habit of making you feel like you owe them something. Isn't it enough that I choose to spend my time with him more regularly now? Why does one always have to *move forward.* What's wrong with being content with the here and now?

I drop my stuff on the floor next to the sofa and sit down, letting the plush cushions envelop me. Home sweet home. At least here I'm free to do whatever the fuck I want.

Closing my eyes for a moment, I try to clear my head, but it's not working. Restless, I sit up and note a blinking light originating inside my handbag on the floor. My phone. *Now what?*

I scroll through the notifications and nearly choke on my breath when I see it's a Facebook friend request from Gareth. Fuck. For years I've enjoyed myself without answering to anyone. Now all of a sudden not just one, but two guys are after me, demanding my attention.

In a moment of weakness I allow myself a quick

glance at his profile. He hasn't changed one bit, except perhaps that the brooding expression that I remember him with has been etched into his features a little deeper than before. Eight years will do that to a person. Neither of us are getting any younger.

There are a couple of familiar names in his friend list, people we used to know, whom I've since lost touch with. It strikes me as weird that he has seemingly popped up from nowhere, after disappearing on me almost a decade ago, but his profile suggests that I'm the odd one out and he's never been away.

After poking around in his life for a few minutes, I check my messages, seeing that he's been in touch here too. Flowers, cards and messages, whatever will be next?

Dear Sally,

If/ when you see this, I hope you'll read on rather than delete this straight away. Please allow me the chance to explain things face-to-face. I can't face another eight years without you.

Gareth

I want to throw my phone across the room. What fucking nerve, to come back begging, in a way putting the blame on me for his pathetic, lonely existence. What an absolute wanker!

That's it. I decide to break my self-imposed rule of never smoking inside my flat and light up. But not even the familiar taste of my Marlboro Lights can soothe me tonight. I get up and put out the cigarette again, discarding it in the ashtray by the tiny balcony in frustration.

The view from up here was one of the main draws of this flat, despite the slightly iffy locale. I normally enjoy the sensation of being so high up and far away from whatever nonsense goes on at ground level. Tonight, my special place to escape it all seems inferior and all I end up doing is pace around the lounge, arms folded, trying to analyse the mess in my head.

If Mark wants things to work out, he's going to have to back off a bit.

If Gareth wants to *explain things,* his reasons have got to be bullet-proof, or he'll wish he never found me. That is, if I give him that chance. Should I?

And what about the whole open relationship thing with Mark? How would that be different from what we do now? Aren't things open already, why tag such a heavy term to the end of it. Does he expect me to disclose who I want to go out with and when? What's to guarantee he won't end up being jealous?

I can't agree to anything like that, especially not with this Gareth bullshit hanging over my head. My instincts may tell me to run from it all, but perhaps it's time to face things head-on.

Best to sleep on it, and think of a solution in the morning. Provided I can get to sleep, that is.

Still restless, I pack a few essentials into the shoulder bag hanging behind the door.

It's times like these I'm grateful for the 24 hour gym around the corner. At this time of night it'll be blissfully quiet; I'll probably be the only person in there. I'll work up a sweat until my mind goes blank, then rush back and crash into bed for a much needed few hours of rest.

✷✷✷

I'm surrounded by a heavy blanket of fog, allowing me only to see about ten feet ahead. Someone is holding my hand, looking over I see that it is Dad, his eyes smiling even if the rest of his features remain straight. He's happy for me, in his own way.

The guests come into view on either side of the aisle. Softly lit, cheerful faces appear in the mist, applauding as I take one step after the other, balancing precariously on white satin heels which threaten to sink into the damp ground.

My heart beats faster as I move forward, staying in tune with the band in the background playing 'Here Comes the Bride'. *It'll only be a matter of minutes before I'm reunited with my soon to be groom.*

Towards my left, Mom grabs my hand and gives it an encouraging squeeze. The tears gathering in the corner of her eyes tell me how proud she is today.

Two, three steps up and I'll have reached the front of the wedding party. Dad lets go of me and stands off to the side, while another hand slips through the crook of my arm, coaxing me closer to the right. The fog has thickened though, so I cannot see his face, only the outline of his broad shoulders, dressed in a dark tailored suit.

Instinctively my left hand finds rest on my stomach, which hides a new life I have only just found out about. Nobody knows, I haven't even been able to tell him yet because we've spent the past two nights apart with our respective parents.

It's unnerving, not knowing how he will react, but something inside me has awoken, the desire to see our child grow from an infant into a toddler, and onward through the years. We'll recognise ourselves and each other in her, creating a permanent bond that cannot be broken. Surely, he can't object to something so beautiful?

Gareth's dad steps up in front of us, holding a bible, which is weird, since neither of us are religious. He starts to speak, but my head is swimming with so many hopes and thoughts that I can't focus on what he's saying. His words merge into the background noise, of people, chatting and laughing.

I'm dizzy, it's probably just morning sickness, but I must soldier on without creating a scene in front of everyone. Still, I'm unsteady on my feet and sway to keep my balance. His hand catches me, propping me up.

"Here, this should take care of the lightheadedness," Mark whispers in my ear.

My head snaps to the right, where he's offering me a basket of bread, which I gladly accept. He's so handsome, of course I'd realised that many times before, but today, on our special day, it's even more apparent.

Gareth's dad acts like nothing has ever happened, furiously speaking some gibberish as the guests look on, mesmerised. Minute after minute passes before I can finally decipher some of what is being said.

"Will you, Sally Irving take Gareth Frances Doyle to be your husband..."

Looking over to my right again, Gareth smiles warmly at me.

"Sorry I slipped away for a moment there, but I had good reason to."

"Well?" his dad asks expectantly. "What will it be?"

I jerk up, bathed in sweat and with a jackhammer going off in my temples. *What the fuck was all that about?* It takes me a while to realise where I am, safely back in bed with the curtains drawn tight to keep out the streetlights down below. In the corner, the alarm clock flips to 4:00.

After breathing a deep sigh of relief, I fall back into the pillows. It was only a dream.

My hand is still resting on my stomach though, as if trying to protect what's left of an old, hopeless fantasy. I know there's nothing there. No life, no hope.

All that fizzled away a long time ago, before I became me.

CHAPTER EIGHT

"Morning." Becky smiles, before continuing to unpack her lunch, ready to go into the staff fridge.

I try to respond, but nothing much comes out, except a cough. After surviving most of the winter without so much as a sniffle, today my body decides it would be funny to develop a cold.

"You look like shit." She takes a step back and cocks her head to the side.

"Thanks, I feel so much better hearing that." My voice has returned, though way more hoarse than normal.

"Thank fuck it's Friday, eh?" Becky gives me a pat on the back and heads to the kitchenette. I hope she's going to bring coffee. I could kill for a cup of coffee right now.

While she's gone, I try to snap out of my fuzzy-headed trance. It's like someone has placed a metal torture helmet over my head and is now putting the screws on tight.

Perhaps I should've stayed home. But calling in sick is not my style, because normally, I'm never sick.

Dazed, I sit down at my desk and switch on my PC, but I'm not quite sure what I'm meant to be doing. My To do list from yesterday still has plenty of unfinished items, but I can't focus on either one of them and so I just sit and stare at nothing.

When Becks finally returns she's trying to carry three cups at a time, and nearly spills everything on the ground.

"Here, I found some pouches of Cold & Flu medicine in the kitchen."

She puts two of the cups in front of me, one smelling suspiciously of lemon, and the coffee I desperately crave. She all but swats my hand away when I try to pick up the latter.

"Have the meds first. If you had bothered to look in a mirror on your way in, you'd understand why."

I grumble something mean and unintelligible, and do as she says. She's probably right, even if I don't like to admit it.

"Don't make a face, you grumpy git, drink it!" she orders.

I can't help it though, the stuff tastes hideous, but somehow I manage to force the rest of it down. My struggle lasts for a painful few minutes, before realising it's starting to take effect already.

If my pounding headache and achy throat aren't enough, I'm having a lot of trouble ignoring the crazy dream I had at night. I've never subscribed to dream interpretation, rejecting it as a rather New Age concept, but this time clearly it meant something.

Guess I've been so confused with stuff lately, that even my subconscious can't decide which way to go. I was going to figure out what to do this morning, but I'm not quite up for it.

Hopefully Mark will be patient enough, letting me

think things through this weekend. I don't think we should meet up until I work it out.

As for Gareth… No matter how hard I try not to go down that rabbit hole, it's impossible to resist.

The dream… We were going to be married- though not at all like how it was going to play out in reality of course. But I was so happy, the dream only reminded me of how I felt when I still thought things would work out between us. I haven't felt that hopeful in ages.

I caught a glimpse of the old me, and now that she's out, it's hard to put her back in her box.

How lovely it must be to go through life like that, like how Becky still is to some extent: despite a failed relationship or two, she still has hope that things will work out in the end. For me, cynicism wins in the end without fail.

Looking over at Becky's desk, I see she's texting as usual, her expression calm and content.

I wish I could have that kind of faith.

Across the office, the odd sniffle and sneeze breaks the silence. I guess I'm not the only one who's infected. Everyone is at their desks, either enjoying their first cup of whatever of the day, or quietly working away at those tasks that were meant to be finished already. You never truly can catch up and stay on top of your work in a place like this. But then you're not expected to.

Thankfully though there isn't any chatter today. I wouldn't have the patience to deal with it either. Apparently, losing one's temper is frowned upon in a professional environment.

Mark stalks out of his office, and towards Cath's desk, holding a bundle of paperwork. He looks magnificent as always, whereas I would like nothing better than to vanish today. No baggage, no bullshit, that's our M.O. Being a red-eyed sniffly mess definitely counts as both.

After he's done talking to Cath, he gives me a wave and nod, which I return rather bleakly.

Please don't come over here, or I'll cough on you.

Thankfully, he returns to his office and closes the door. Fridays tend to be busy for everyone, especially him.

My headache lifts slightly further, I like to think it's due to finally being allowed my much needed coffee, and I randomly pick one of today's pending tasks to start with: put together a sales forecast, oh joy.

The morning passes by rather slowly, mainly because my condition seems to be worsening again. By lunchtime, I decide I've had enough and knock on Mark's door.

"Come in," he says.

"Hey…" I'm suddenly torn between wanting to come across all perfect for the Mark I share my bed with, as opposed to needing to play up the miserable sick angle for Mark, the boss.

"Are you alright?" He gets up and lifts my chin towards him.

"Not really, you might want to keep your distance if you don't want to catch it," I say, backing away.

"Don't be stupid. Do you need anything? You

should probably go home and rest. I can come by after work to check on you." His voice sounds so warm and inviting, it's making my chest feel tight.

After spending most of the morning feeling sorry for myself, I hate to admit that I really could use some TLC. Just a hug would be nice even. But I can't accept his offer, if I did, it would mean I'm agreeing to something else also. I can't do that, my mind is racing again and I'm almost suffocating with more than just a congested chest.

"Uhh no, that's the other thing I wanted to say. Perhaps it's best we have some distance while I figure everything out."

His expression falls, and he backs away, sitting down on his chair again.

"If that's what you want."

"That's it, I don't know what I want. Except a nap. I really want a nap right now."

"Just let Cath know on your way out and get Becky to take over any urgent accounts."

It stings, the realisation that I've basically shot him down while he was trying to be nice and caring. I'm no good at letting people care for me. They inevitably let you down when you need them the most, so it's best not to rely on anyone.

"OK thanks, Mark," I mumble, while letting myself out of his office.

I don't know how we'll ever be OK again.

* * *

By the time I reach my place, I feel deflated and empty. It occurs to me I should probably have lunch before crashing into bed, but I can't be arsed to do anything about it. My cupboards are pretty much barren, as is the fridge. Who the hell even delivers takeout at this time of day?

I grab a bunch of sweets leftover from Christmas and get cosy under the covers.

For hours I'm drifting in and out of sleep, until I finally get up at nine, starving and aching all over.

Now I really wish I hadn't told Mark to stay away. If nothing else, he would've brought food or could've made me something. But it's too late for that now, and a quick check of my phone reveals he's not on chat either.

Plus, it's not like I could do or say anything to him now to make things better. He'll be pissed at me, and with good reason too.

Just when I want to put the phone away again, something makes me open up Gareth's message from last night again. Would it be so bad to meet him once? Now that he's haunting me in my dreams again for the first time in years, I've got to do *something* to make it stop.

He broke me once, and I have to believe I'm stronger now.

Once he says whatever it is he has to say, I'll know why things turned out the way they did. I'll understand why he left me.

And then I can tell him to fuck off in person.

OK fine. Come to the White Hart on Bath Road. Monday, 7pm.
Sally

I hit send before I have the chance to change my mind.

CHAPTER NINE

I reluctantly wait by the pub entrance, scanning the crowd for Gareth. He better not have stood me up this time, after practically begging to meet! I'm in a good mind to turn around as it is.

A figure, in the same old leather jacket I spied at the office earlier this week turns away from the bar, holding two drinks, and I'm stopped in my tracks. *Fuck.* There he is.

He shoots me a tentative smile, and nods over at some empty seats by the window, away from most of the commotion in the place. I cut across the room, as does he, until we meet on opposite sides of the round wooden table.

"Hi," he says.

I just nod. I may have drugged myself heavily with various over-the-counter concoctions to get here, but I'm not yet convinced they'll have worked on my voice. Only two hours ago, I sounded barely any better than a creaking door. Perhaps I should have cancelled, after all I suggested tonight thinking I'd be better by now. Then again I'm just keen to get it all over with.

We sit down, not knowing what else to do and stare at each other for a moment. This is so weird. I want to be angry at him, ask him what the fuck was wrong with him to let me down so badly eight years ago, but suddenly I'm more intrigued than pissed off.

And awkward. Mainly I'm feeling super awkward.

"You look great," he remarks, finally.

"Thanks." Thank fuck, my voice works again.

"I got you a rum & coke. You always used to like those." He slides one of the two identical tall glasses towards me.

I don't say anything, just nod, no point telling him now that my tastes have developed a bit during our time apart. But he still seems the same. I spent years trying to reinvent myself, assuming it's a process everyone goes through growing up. Perhaps I was wrong.

The bit of stubble on his chin, messy brown hair, the blue piercing eyes which could see right into my soul - or so I thought when I was a stupid teenager - he's exactly how I remember him. Even down to the jacket, paired with faded jeans and biker boots. No wonder Elaine was so taken with him after he came to work, he does still have that bad boy charm around him. *But I'm so over all that!*

I don't know whether to cut right to it, or let him lead the conversation for a bit. Being in his presence again after such a long time is making me unsure of a lot of stuff.

"So… how have you been? Had a good holiday?" He smiles again, awkwardly, and we clink our drinks together before taking our first sips.

"Fine. Very well actually. Things have been great." I don't think that sounded convincing, but somehow, I really do want to make it a point that I did just fine without him, or anyone. "You?"

"Yeah… No, I can't say the same. It's been a rough few years." He fishes the lemon wedge out of his drink and squeezes a few drops of juice out of it. That old habit of his used to annoy me even back then, but I don't comment.

"So to what do I owe this sudden pleasure?" I say.

"It took me a while to track you down. You'd pretty much vanished after… " I stare at him, daring him to finish that sentence. I pretty much vanished, after he fucking vanished first, but still, I bite my tongue.

"About that, I have been curious how you managed it. I've not kept in touch with anyone from back in the day."

He smiles briefly, then averts his gaze.

"It's all a lot easier nowadays, with the internet and all."

"Uhuh." I get the feeling there's something he's leaving unsaid.

"Well anyway, I just wanted to let you know that I never meant for things to end the way they did. I was in a bad place back then." He runs his hands through his hair, something he always used to do when nervous.

I press my lips together, trying to prevent any rash remarks from passing through.

"Neither did I, and yet, they did end." *And who's fault is that?* I take another, bigger sip this time, glad that he at least ordered me a double.

"You know, that day-" He pauses, stares down at my hand on my glass.

"What about it?"

"I got arrested. That's why I didn't turn up." His eyes flick up at me, and for the first time I think I see regret.

"Right." *That's the big reason? What a load of shit.*

"They got me for that time I was out with Roy and Luke and we nicked that car off old Mr. Teesdale and went for a little drive around town. We intended to park it back in its place, but by the time we had had our fun, there were cops everywhere so we dumped it and ran."

I take a deep breath, and rub my temples. My fingertips are nearly frozen from holding on to the cold drink. I don't know if it's my cold, or talking to Gareth after so long, perhaps both, but my head is swimming again.

"You couldn't have called? Sent someone to let me know? I was waiting around the registrar's office like a total idiot, until finally they took pity on me and made me a cup of tea..."

I remember the thing with the old guy's car. As soon as I heard about it, I had wanted to lop Gareth over the head with the nearest blunt object. Those two assholes he chose to hang out with had always been trouble.

"I tried to, I called Karen, but she told me to piss off and that you'd be better off without me anyway."

With the mention of my cousin and our mutual 'friend' Karen things start to fall into place. That sounds like her, the meddling bitch. As I recall, she always had a thing for him, so obviously she would welcome the chance to break us up. But to think that it actually worked is too much.

"So that was that then?" I hate this sinking feeling in my chest, like I'm being let down again when I had tried so hard not to go into this with any expectations whatsoever. Perhaps, if only subconsciously, I had hoped for something more. That the worst day of my life would have been caused by something a bit more substantial.

"I figured she was probably right."

"And my opinion didn't matter anymore, yeah?"

"By the time I realised I made a huge mistake, you were nowhere to be found. I've regretted it every single day."

Even though the last part sounds genuine enough, and he's put his best guilty face on, I can't contain my frustration. My cheeks glow and my breathing has turned ragged as a result of the anger burning up inside my chest. I can't believe I suffered so much pain because of something so stupid.

"Should've thought of that sooner." I push my chair back, take another two big gulps from the drink, suffering severe brain freeze as a consequence, but I don't care. I've had enough of this shit and need to get away. Suddenly the pub atmosphere is not cosy, as probably intended by the landlord, but instead it threatens to suffocate me.

"Wait, Sally!" He jumps up as well, and tries to squeeze through some of the chairs blocking him in, but I don't stand around and wait. I make a beeline for the exit, nearly hitting into a group of girls in skimpy dresses, much like the type I would wear, before I hit my mid-twenties and discovered that I could sense the cold after all.

After that near-accident, nothing stands between me and the door. I need air.

Outside, I get out my packet of cigarettes, noticing the unwelcome shakiness in my fingers. Never in the past eight years have I let anyone affect me like this. But all this old shit being dragged back up is making my defences crumble at every instance. That's why the awkwardness with Mark has been so rough as well: I'm totally off my game. It's unacceptable.

I light up and inhale deeply, waiting for the nicotine to do its job.

Gareth has finally made it out as well, and notices me quickly enough. I'm in a good mind to run, but he'd catch me. And I guess I do have to finish this conversation somehow.

"Hey! I thought you were going to up and disappear again." He leans against the wall next to me and observes me as I take another drag. If he says a word about how I never used to smoke, I'll put it out in his fucking face.

"You didn't expect that once I listen to that story of yours everything would be forgiven?"

"Uhh, no I guess not. But how things ended between us has really bothered me and I couldn't just leave things as they were." It *really bothered* him? That's the best he can come up with?

"I gave up everything to be with you, to make a life with you. And you threw it away for some shit Karen said?"

"I…" He shifts uncomfortably from one foot to the other. "She did make a solid point. There I was, being held for stealing a car - which by the way they never did catch Luke or Roy for, only me - meanwhile you were giving up on going to university for me. Without me, you could make something of yourself. I didn't even know whether I'd be looking at being locked up or just a warning or what."

Put like that, I suppose I can see where he's coming from. But if he had wanted to somehow save me from what a life with him would entail, wouldn't it have been better to give me a choice in the matter?

"You have no idea what you did that day." I throw the cigarette butt down and stomp on it repeatedly, releasing some of my anger, until everything down to the filter is destroyed and mushed into the moist pavement.

"Clearly not. They let me out the following day and I went looking for you, went by your folks where your Dad nearly beat the shit out of me. They thought you'd left with me as planned. Nobody knew where you were."

"Of course they didn't! What was I supposed to do? After weeks of arguments, I had packed my shit, emptied my savings account and left, leaving only a note. I couldn't very well turn back and say *'Oh, things didn't work out with Gareth, just like you said they wouldn't, can I move back in now?'* I snort in outrage. "And after they obviously welcomed me with *open arms,* I'd add: *'By the way, Mum, Dad, I'm pregnant.'* That would've gone down *so well* with them."

Throughout my rant, I hadn't noticed the tears streaming down my face.

I hadn't told a soul the whole story of what happened that day. After waiting all day I ran, not to London like we'd agreed, instead I boarded the first train I saw. In the end I wouldn't have known where I ended up but for the sign at the final station: Newtowne, a bland 1970s commuter town which has nothing much going for it. Mainly, I wanted to get away from everything I guess. Everything and everyone. And I couldn't imagine anyone would think to follow me *here.*

Gareth's expression is one of utter shock. His mouth is half open and eyes are about ready to pop out.

"So it's true," he finally says, blinking a few times.

"What?" I'm doing my best to dry my eyes, but it's no use. All my defences have finally crumbled.

"Karen said-" I shoot him a mean glance through wet lashes at the mention of that backstabbing bitch but he ignores me. "Fuck. You really were pregnant."

"I never told anyone, especially her."

"She guessed it, anyway, that's not the point. Where is it? Where's the child?"

I can't stop the flow of tears, and try to hide my face which must be streaky and hideously patchy by now.

"How could you let me down like that? I had nobody else but you, you know that. It was supposed to be us against the world." Hearing those words spoken in my own voice opens the floodgates for deeper, more desperate sobs.

He grabs me by both my arms, his warmth piercing starkly through the surrounding cold and I start to shiver uncontrollably. For a moment, I'm swept up by the thought that perhaps this is one of those stupid, crazy reconciliations you get at the end of a romance novel. That just maybe, through his touch which I had so intensely craved for years, I could overcome all the pain he's caused me. Still, I'm a puddle of overwhelming emotions and lean into him slightly, trying to reclaim my balance.

"Where is it?" he repeats.

I look up, trying to blink the watery haze away.

"Where's what?"

"*My* child." His features have hardened, and his fingers are digging in harder now. The deliberate emphasis in his demand gives me pause.

"There is no child." I sniffle, and try to reach up to check that my nose isn't starting to drip, but he refuses to loosen his grip.

"What do you mean, you just said you were pregnant." Both his eyes have narrowed, he's getting annoyed.

"I miscarried a few months later," I stammer, taken aback by the sudden change in his mood.

"Fuck." He lets go and balls his fists hard enough I can hear his knuckles crack.

"Is that what this was about? You tracked me down thinking I had your baby?" I take a step back, and wipe my face dry once and for all. *Enough*. I've had enough of the drama, enough of the stories, the fucking emotions. How dare he?

"Answer me!" Again, I've got that sinking feeling of not only disappointment now, but betrayal.

"What do you think? I'd find out about something so major and not investigate? Karen said-"

"What's with Karen this, Karen that? You two seem to be awfully chummy!"

He throws me a cold glance. I understand now.

"You've been fucking Karen ever since, haven't you? That's why you never tried to come after me until now." I take a deep breath, aiming not to let the growing rage inside my belly boil over. I'm shaking again, but not due to cold or painful memories. My muscles tighten with a sudden surge in adrenalin.

"We've been an item, yes."

"And for whatever reason, she told you I had your baby? Jesus fucking Christ. You really are a dumb shit, Gareth!"

"Keep your voice down, I'm telling you!" he spits through gritted teeth.

"You don't get to tell me a fucking thing, Gareth! As far as I'm concerned all this shit is done and over with. Why don't you run along home to *Karen*. You two deserve each other."

He steps forward to grab me again, my own rage reflected in his eyes.

"Bitch, I didn't come all this way to be humiliated in public by some whore, who thinks it's below her to give people a chance. Who just cuts and runs at the first sign of trouble and leaves behind all those who care about her." His hand locks around my wrist again, so tight the blood flow to my fingers is starting to slow.

"Oh hell no! This shit may fly with my cousin, but you're not laying a finger on me!"

From the corner of my eye, I see some bystanders shuffle around uncomfortably, uncertain whether to intervene. I look towards the door of the pub, wondering if their bouncer has started his shift yet, but there's no sign of anyone who fits the bill. He takes a step forward until his face is mere inches away from mine. I wonder what he's going to do next. Gareth has always had a temper, even back then. But I refuse to let him faze me.

"Let go of me or you'll regret it." I stare straight at him, into those blue eyes that used to mean something to me, which now just seem empty and unimportant.

He doesn't react, not instantly, until out of nowhere, a hand, adorned with a couple of oriental silver rings and bright red nail polish wraps itself around Gareth's throat.

"Get your hands off her," a familiar voice threatens, as Gareth stumbles backwards.

Holy fucking shit.

CHAPTER TEN : MARK

The first time I saw the guy, my understanding of what I felt for Sally changed. The second time, it changed my understanding of who she was, really.

Not only was she infuriatingly independent, to the extent that she pretended not to need a soul around her. This part I had already understood before, which had pretty much made me give up on trying to win her over. She also had a softer, vulnerable side which I'd never seen before.

When she basically told me to piss off on Friday, I was in a good mood to shut her out of my life completely. If she wanted things to be like that, I would tolerate her at the office somehow, then get on with life on my own. For years I've hidden a significant part of myself from the world, which has made me a good liar. I'd learnt to lie to myself pretty well too.

I had tried to show what I could offer her. If it took more than a traditional relationship, then I'd find a way of sharing her with other people. But I needed to put a label on it. I needed to reassure myself that she wouldn't just up and leave without so much as an explanation. I needed a commitment.

If any of my exes knew about this, they'd find it hard to contain their laughter. I had never wanted a commitment before Sally.

But to see that creep threaten her in public made me

see red. I forgot that I was angry at her. That I had vowed not to let her get under my skin again because we had no hope in hell of making it work. I threw caution in the wind, and followed my instincts.

I even forgot that I was wearing stiletto heels and a cocktail dress.

When I realised, it was too late. Sally's mouth hung open in shock, and she could not stop staring at me while I held Gareth in a headlock.

I totally fucked up.

That's when the cops turned up and shoved her and me into one of those fortified vans you often see parked around the town centre at night, before stuffing Gareth by himself into the back of their car.

"Umm…" Sally breaks the silence inside the dark mobile holding cell.

I don't respond, but keep on sitting there, with my head in my hands. Holy hell, this is awkward as awkward can be. In all the years I've allowed myself the occasional night out fully dressed up, I've always been super careful not to go near where I know people from work hang out. Despite living in a relatively small city, with few places to go, I'd never been made.

There are a few noises, some shuffling around at the far side of the van where I know she is, followed by footsteps.

"I'm really sorry," Sally says.

I flinch when her hand rests on my shoulder. Her touch always has caused me to react intensely, but now that the game is up, it's not arousal that I feel but shame. It's a lot easier to convince yourself you have nothing to be ashamed of when nobody you know has seen you femmed up.

"He didn't hurt you, did he?" she asks.

I shake my head. Gareth tried to get a few punches in while I tried to pry him away from her, but the only casualties in this fight were a couple of my fingernails.

There's more silence between us, it's painful to wait through it for what I know will come next: awkward questions or remarks. If I'm lucky she'll assume I was going to a fancy dress party.

She sits down next to me, so close I can sense the warmth of her thigh radiate against mine.

"So…" she pauses.

I sigh, waiting for the inevitable.

"What's your name?"

I look up, confused. Is she in denial? Surely, she must have recognised me.

"I mean - and I may be way off - but I thought perhaps you'd use a different name. When you're dressed like this I mean." She blinks nervously, then looks away.

Though this is obviously uncomfortable, she seems more intrigued than put off.

"Melody. I tend to go by Melody."

"Nice. I like it." She smiles briefly, without making eye contact, then fidgets with the buttons on her coat. "It would've been weird, calling you Mark. That would sort of ruin it, wouldn't it?"

Recognising her question as rhetorical, I remain

quiet. Anyway, I'm not sure what to say to her. This whole situation is way too similar to many nightmares I've had, which inevitably end up in humiliation. I'd never seriously considered coming out to someone I know. Perhaps if I'd given it more thought, I would have prepared a few lines. While in my job I could steer any conversation in exactly the direction I want, this is completely beyond my skills.

"Love your shoes," she says.

I look down at the buckled black leather boots on my feet. My favourites for this time of year.

"Thanks," I mumble. I feel like telling her I've always loved her choice of shoes, clothes, whatever. I want to respond that it means a lot to have her approval, but it would only sound desperate, so I keep quiet.

"I wonder how long they'll keep us in here. Clearly it was all *his* fault." Sally leans back, sighing and rubbing her forehead with the back of her hand.

Earlier, when I came across the both of them, she was staring him down despite the obvious imbalance in size and strength: he was a good foot taller than her.

Perhaps when facing off with him, she felt there was nothing more he could do to her, like she had nothing to lose. Perhaps it wasn't the first time he'd been violent with her and she'd had enough? The thought infuriates me again, causing me to tense up. I'd tried to stay composed, and only do the needful but if pushed, I would have been capable of inflicting permanent damage on the guy. Still am.

"I probably owe you an explanation, huh?" Sally

leans forward again, resting her elbows on her knees.

"Not really. It's none of my business."

"I know you were jealous when he turned up at work, but there's nothing going on between us, at least not anymore…" She rubs her hands together, and attempts to blow some warmth into them.

"I wasn't-"

"That's not what Cath said." Hell yeah I was jealous, who wouldn't be? It just seems impossible to admit now.

I glance over, and she returns my gaze. She's so different than the Sally I thought I knew. Of course I never truly got to know her, which is possibly my own fucking fault, but still. She seems smaller, more fragile than I'd ever seen her before.

"Gareth and I were together back when I was just a teenager. It didn't work out."

I wonder whether to ask questions. Like whether she'd left him because he hit her, but it really does seem like I'm better off not knowing.

"Actually, that's not the whole story. He practically left me at the altar - registrar's office - same thing. This whole business with him tracking me down… I dunno…" She sniffles and rubs her forehead again. "He said he wanted to explain what happened, to apologise. But I think it was bullshit, all of it."

"Was he always such a tool?" I wonder out loud.

"I've been asking myself that too." She lets out a half-hearted chuckle.

I reach over, covering her hands with mine. They're

freezing, of course. Putting on the fucking heating in this van would've been too much trouble for the noble protectors of the law who put us here.

Her fingers thread through mine, and for a moment there, it doesn't seem to matter what happened tonight, or over the past few weeks, or even ages ago between her and Gareth. If we ever get out of here, I just want to take care of her as long as she'll let me, even if I only get to be a friend.

She leans against me, her head on my shoulder, until we're interrupted by some commotion outside.

"Alright," a gruff voice barks right outside the metal doors at the far end of the van. "Mrs. Doubtfire and the girl can leave now." A couple more voices snigger at his remark.

We share a look, while the locks creak and groan and the door opens, letting in a waft of even colder air.

"After making further inquiries and interviewing witnesses of the incident," the skinny policeman who initially held us says, "we could confirm that you were indeed acting in self defence against a-" He nods down at his notebook. "Gareth Doyle, who has a history of violent behaviour including assault resulting in grievous injury." The cop puts his notebook into his coat pocket and steps aside to let us exit the van.

"You're free to go."

"Thanks," I grumble, while getting up.

Sally doesn't say a word, just holds on tightly to my hand. I note she's begun shivering violently, so I put my arm around her shoulder and pull her against me while we walk off towards the nearest taxi stand, leaving the bemused policemen and various bystanders behind.

CHAPTER ELEVEN

What a fucking night.

I should have listened to my gut and not met Gareth. Then again, if I hadn't, I wouldn't have ended up here at Mark's place tonight. Or should I say Melody's place? Over towards the open plan kitchen, I can see him - her - zipping back and forth from counter to stove and back to the fridge, the black flowy fabric of her dress, exaggerating every movement.

The moment we reached back, I was consigned to the sofa, where I was to stay under any circumstance, under various warm blankets. Apparently this is how you catch pneumonia: by going out on a particularly frosty January night and ending up in an unheated police van. Although I'm still sceptical about the dangers of getting a little cold while having the sniffles, I was shivering so badly, I wasn't able or willing to argue.

I wonder how many people have stories like this to tell; tonight had started off so seemingly normal as well.

The room is starting to smell rather lovely, and I don't recall eating anything proper all weekend. To be fair I don't know how I actually survived those two days, and today at the office, consuming mainly Paracetamol and caffeinated liquids.

"Have this while I make the soup," Ma-Melody says, putting a steaming cup of herbal tea on the coffee table in front of the couch.

"Thanks."

It's all a tad surreal, finding a six foot amazonian brunette come to your aid in an escalating row with an ex you haven't seen in years. It's even more surreal recognising said brunette as your on-and-off lover and full-time boss. Thinking back, it's obvious Mark had secrets. I just thought they came in the form of *another person* with a penchant for lacey underwear and long fingernails. It's funny how life turns out sometimes.

I pick up the cup, coughing profusely when the steamy fumes hit my nose. Fucking hell. I hate being sick.

"If it tastes weird, add some honey," *Melody* says.

I wrinkle my nose at the thought, I'm more of a black coffee kind of person, but apparently I'm in need of the benefits of this particular concoction of greenery. Mint and echyna-something. I never could pronounce that one. And anyway, flowers aren't food in my mind.

Fine. If it makes *Melody* happy, I'll drink the stuff. If it makes me feel better, that'll be an added bonus.

The pounding headache that worsened after we got almost-arrested is starting to subside. Tonight generally has been an overdose of emotions and surprises. Gareth can so fuck off right now. And when he gets there, he can fuck off some more...

As I confronted him about all the shit I went through after he basically abandoned me, I started to realise that for years I haven't truly allowed myself to feel. I hadn't dealt with the negative shit, and as a result, couldn't appreciate the positive either.

During that little moment of weakness when I thought I craved his touch, actually, he wasn't who I was yearning for. I did want a connection with someone. When *Melody* turned up, and we were put in that metal box together, I finally understood that I wasn't the only one with secrets.

I was hiding a past, in which I honestly believed I could create a family with an asshole like Gareth, only to be crushed when things didn't work out quite how I had hoped. Mark had been hiding an entire side of his current self.

As scared as I had felt, opening up my weaknesses even to Becky, who I trust despite our vast differences, I couldn't imagine how he must have felt. I couldn't have known of course, but I felt ashamed that I'd brought up those little details I found, that evidence of his other life, during our argument last week.

I unknowingly poked around in something I didn't understand, something so private he wasn't ready to share. Just like how I hadn't been ready to share my secrets with him.

Yet all that stuff was forced out into the open, for better or for worse.

Melody is now rummaging around in a cupboard, retrieving two bowls and a tray. I watch her as she moves with a certain elegance Mark doesn't normally display. Or perhaps it's only my perception that has changed.

I had wanted to say that I was OK with it, back in the van. But it didn't seem like the right time, so I just tried to act cool.

"Here." Melody puts one bowl on the table in front of me and the other nearer the armchair towards my left.

"Thanks. That smells amazing." I smile, grateful for the chance to put the suspiciously green herbal tea back down.

"Nothing fancy, it's only chicken soup."

"I couldn't cook chicken soup to save my life," I remark.

She nods at me, a knowing grin on her face.

"Yeah, that's pretty obvious."

I smile back at her, marvelling at the transformation that can be achieved with a bit of makeup, a wig and a nice outfit. She's beautiful, not *OK-for-a-dude-in-a-dress,* but genuinely so. Meanwhile, I spent a good part of the evening looking like a scarecrow with Kiss style face paint on. It was a relief to be able to ask for makeup remover once we got here. Funny, how natural it is to act as if I'm at a girlfriend's house all of a sudden.

"If I had known you have so many nice things." I nod at Melody's handbag on the table. "I might have asked to borrow some of them."

"Perhaps then it's a good thing you didn't know." She winks at me, and starts eating her soup.

Although I never actually said anything to cut through the tension, things seem more relaxed now. We're alone, away from prying eyes, free to be ourselves.

Yet I can't take my eyes off her, although I'm trying

not to stare. Suddenly aware, Melody looks up from her bowl, wearing a concerned frown.

"If it's too weird, I can - you know - change…"

Shit, busted! I quickly shake my head, aware that unusually, I can't afford to play coy. There is too much of a risk for misunderstandings right now.

"No, no, it's not that." I glance down at the steamy bowl for a moment, nerves surging. Shit, how do I put this? "I just think you look really beautiful."

Her expressions changes, but only subtly, as we maintain eye contact. A bit of a smile plays on her lips, but it's too faint to be certain, while my heart hammers away inside my chest.

"Thanks." She blinks, trying to hide the beginnings of tears in her eyes.

I sit up straighter and put my soup down. It's hard to find the right words, when it seems like so much depends on the here and now. No wonder first dates are meant to be so difficult. You go into the situation hoping for the best possible outcome, at a time when things are at their most fragile. Why is it so damn impossible to find the right thing to say?

"So you don't think it's weird?" she asks.

"Not really. It's certainly different, seeing you like this," I say, regretting my phrasing as soon as she frowns again. "Shit, that didn't come out right. I mean, it's like that being with two people, rather than just one. Does that make sense?"

"I suppose so."

We quietly finish our soup, after which she collects

the dirty dishes and leaves them in the kitchen. I wonder if I fucked up and ruined what little progress we'd made so far.

It's only nine, too early to turn in for the night, though both my health and today's exertions are still catching up with me, exhausting me.

When she's back after filling up the dishwasher, Melody leans over and touches my forehead with the back of her hand. I close my eyes, trying to will my heartbeat to slow down but it's no use. Although I've often felt giddy in Mark's company, that was nothing compared to what's going on now.

"Don't think you've got a fever," she remarks. "But it would be a bad idea for you should head out into the cold anyway."

I breathe a sigh of relief. Although things are still pretty awkward, I have no wish to leave now. The only way through this weirdness is forward.

"I'd like to stay with you if that's OK."

She smiles at me.

"Of course."

I wonder if my intention shone through: I didn't mean on the couch. Her hand still lingers on my forehead, and I take it, searching for agreement in her eyes. She gently closes her fingers around mine, causing the hairs at the back of my neck to stand up. I hold my breath as I caress her with my fingertips.

"I'm so sorry I've been such a bitch lately. I hope you'll forgive me?" I ask, more desperate than ever for things to be OK between us.

Melody sits down on the armrest beside me, and I lean up against the cushions, waiting for her response.

"It's fine. It's not like I've been totally upfront." She hesitates, as if wanting to say something more, but then just reaches out and plays with a lock of my hair.

I rest my head against her thigh, noting how she flinches slightly again, like when I first touched her shoulder in the police van. But neither of us pull away, and soon, her hand finds more locks, caressing and untangling them, while I continue to hold her other hand.

If my nerves are anything to go by, how must she feel?

"I don't want to infect you with my germs…" I say. *But I really want to kiss you.*

"I don't care."

I half-turn, and find her already staring down at me. The tension between us is so intense, it's incomparable with anything I've ever felt before, whether with Mark or anyone else.

"May I?" I ask, reaching for the side of her face.

Melody closes her eyes and nods, and I let my thumb brush over her lower lip. I cast aside the throws and blankets and get up, only to kneel on the sofa, facing her.

Neither of us want to wait any longer. Her fingers thread through my locks, guiding me closer, and my lips hungrily meet hers. Our lips part almost instantly, allowing our kisses to deepen, and some of the uncertainty from before to fade. But there's still this tension, this growing need inside me to go further.

I want her with all my being.

The frantic dance our tongues have entered into tells me she wants the same.

I stare into her eyes to find that they're open again, naked and honest in amber. For once I understand when people say they can tell just from a look what the other person is thinking. Maybe I hadn't been looking hard enough, or I wasn't ready to see what was there all along.

Finally, I know all there is to know. I can plainly see her for who she is, and can't stop the urge to drown in those eyes.

"Come closer," I whisper.

Melody slides off the armrest, and kneels right in front of me, our bodies as close as we can manage. I start caressing her, exploring the contours of the body I thought I knew so well. Her toned shoulders, which I'd thought quite strong and masculine before, now seem fitting with her new persona. She's certainly not a dainty female, her height has made that an impossibility, but nothing is out of place. Her physique is more akin to a warrior princess whereas I'm weak and insignificant in comparison.

Her sides seem to curve like one would expect on a woman, even if her hips aren't as rounded as mine. I reach around, feeling for the zip of her dress, while she unbuttons my skinny jeans.

Once I manage to open it, she hesitates for a moment, searching for confirmation in my eyes, but finally lets the smooth black fabric slide off her to reveal what looks like a plain black sports bra.

This is the secret, what makes Melody Melody. The cup size she's chosen is again perfect for her athletic frame.

Leaning in, I cover what bare skin I can find with kisses, before running my fingers over the swell in her bra. Melody holds her breath, closing her eyes again. I continue to tease, explore and play, like how I would want it. I know how to treat a girl, it's not the first time. I wonder if it's the first time for her?

"You're beautiful," I mumble, while nuzzling her neck and nibbling gently on her skin. It must tickle, judging by how her head snaps to the side, almost trapping me, but she does not protest.

"You're not just saying that?" she whispers, between the short staccato of her excited breaths.

"Hell no." I try drown out any further concerns with further kisses lavishing her lips.

"I've never... you know... while dressed," Melody answers my unspoken question.

Where earlier I had felt feverish and lethargic, I'm filled with a renewed energy. What I'm doing here, to her, is special. And because of it, and our changed dynamic, I'm beside myself with desire.

"That's about to change, if you want..." I say.

She smiles into my kisses, and responds by removing my top. That's all the encouragement I need to get on my back, and wriggle out and discard the rest of my clothes.

How different things are, compared to the last time we found ourselves here on this sofa. Different and so much better.

Running my hands down her flat, toned stomach, I reach the lacey edge of her panties. The soft stretchy fabric is straining to contain the one thing I do know very well about her. I cup the bulge gently, and circle around, ever inwards with my fingernail.

"Tell me how you like it, Melody," I say.

Her eyes light up, as her breathing stocks with every movement of my fingers. I'm about ready to burst myself, and the same seems true for her.

"Gently," she mouths, almost inaudibly.

I take her by the hand, prompting her to turn 90 degrees until her stockinged legs are resting on those gorgeous heeled boots on the floor, and straddle her. Something tells me she wants to keep her panties on, so instead of undressing her further, I slip her solid cock out from the side. Taking it in my hand, I wrap my fingers around and massage, gently, but firmly enough to have an effect.

All the memories I have, of fun-filled nights involving activities much like this pale in comparison with the passion that has grown inside me. I could scream, not out of pain or frustration, but out of joy, I'm that grateful for how things have turned out.

But before I voice any of that, it's time to take the step: to take Melody's virginity.

I lower myself onto her, enjoying the familiar sensation of her length filling me. The fabric of her panties, though noticeable, does not detract from the experience. Instead it rubs my clit just right.

She moans softly into my ear, her hands close around my hips until they've stopped trembling.

"This… is so perfect." Melody runs one hand up all the way over my back until it reaches my neck and she pulls me in closer.

"I agree. Perfect," I respond.

I rock back and forth, gently as requested, my hands continuing to enjoy the softness of her breasts, which are surprisingly realistic. Until I can't hold back anymore, and speed up, coaxed along by her hold on my ass. Our bodies are joined, entwined, like they've never been before. Like I know when to push down, when to flick my hips to heighten her pleasure, along with my own. She digs her fingers in deep into my flesh, moaning almost continuously, as my own release is so achingly close I can almost taste it.

I fight the lethargy that threatens to return, struggle through the weakness in my aching limbs, focus only on her breaths and gasps and the sweet tickle in the bottom of my abdomen.

Two, three thrusts more, and I've nearly reached the summit, yet I power on to take her with me.

Sweat starts to collect on my brow, a sign of my continued efforts, and I'm dangerously close to the point of no return when she joins in, arms wrapped around me tightly and hips twitching feverishly upwards into me. I cry out, and try to hang on in a vice-like embrace as she finishes us both in an explosion of sweet relief.

I collapse on top of her, lost for words as well as breath. All I can think to do is just to hide my face in the crook of her neck, enjoying the tickle of her hair on my cheek. She holds me in her arms, caressing my hair until we've both calmed ourselves.

Time passes, but we don't stir. I don't want to give this up, this moment, and this closeness. Now I understand how very dear she - he - is to me. It's been hard-fought, us coming together like this. A lot has happened, we've both been hurt, and needed mending first. I hope this is the first step of many, to make things right again.

"I feel like I've met you for the first time tonight," a voice that sounds deceptively like Mark says.

He takes off his long wig, as well as the pretty earrings I had admired earlier. I lean up, finding him already staring at me. My heart skips a beat, though I'm not quite sure why.

"I know the feeling."

His eyes soften, as he lets his gaze linger on me a bit longer before continuing.

"You never told me you like girls." He winks at me, like he often does when he's trying to tease me.

"You never asked." I take a deep breath, forcing myself out of character, to add something more heartfelt. "Plus it would seem that Melody isn't just any girl, but someone rather special."

Mark pauses for a moment, then brushes a few strands of my damp hair out of my face.

"How about I get changed, and you finish that tea and get into bed. At this rate, you'll really catch something nasty."

I press my lips together, trying to hide my disappointment that he noticed I didn't finish my cup of whatever herbal nonsense. The look he's giving me, so full of concern is impossible to ignore though, so I decide to play along.

"Let's hope you don't catch the same thing," I mumble, while struggling up and reaching over to retrieve the half full cup. It's barely luke-warm by now so I neck it, trying to ignore the taste.

Behind me, the rustle of fabrics suggests he's getting up and gathering our various clothes. Then unexpectedly, his arms reach around my back and the back of my knees and I'm lifted into the air before I can do anything about it.

"I mean it, off to bed with you. You're not going anywhere until you're well again."

I feel like arguing, want to say I've done just fine on my own for the past few years, thank-you-very-much, but I bite my tongue instead and wrap my arms around his neck. He can have this one. Right now, there's no place I'd rather spend the night than in his bed.

EPILOGUE

I wrap myself tighter in my fur trimmed coat, the one I wore the first time Mark and I met, and gaze up at the magnificent sight of the Eiffel Tower ahead of us. Mark steps up behind me, and rests his arm around my shoulders, which I gratefully lean back into.

Despite darkness already having set over the city, there are so many lights, so much to see. The entire tower is tastefully lit up as well, serving as a shining beacon against the crisp, starry sky.

"If you want, we can take a lift all the way up and have dinner in the panoramic restaurant."

The prospect makes me smile.

"That would be amazing, but I'm sure they'll be full. Plus I'm not quite dressed for the occasion."

"It's the middle of winter, what do they expect?"

"Some Parisian woman with legs all the way to her waist, in a designer dress with minimum coverage that perfectly matches her Christian Louboutins?"

A gust of wind reminds me that even though I'm in jeans and a sweater underneath the heavy coat, it's still not quite enough to counter the elements today.

"They can go to hell if that's the only way to get in. Let's see if we can get a table." He pulls me tighter towards him as we walk off to the base of the tower, narrowly avoiding the odd souvenir salesman trying to flog us his wares.

This trip is already special enough, I don't need a shiny golden Eiffel tower replica to remind me of it later. As far as mementos go, I've got the best one already: a sketched portrait of us, done by an artist we came across in Montmartre yesterday.

When we asked for another addition to the scene, showing him a picture of *Melody*, he simply shrugged and added her without saying a word. I'm sure he's had weirder requests in the past.

I wait off to the side from the lift entrance, while Mark makes his enquiries regarding the restaurant. It'll be a fucking miracle if he manages to get us in tonight, on Valentine's day. But sure enough, the doorman nods, and Mark gives me a little wave.

"Let's go. It'll give us a chance to warm up."

As I walk past, the doorman ticks off an entry in his notebook. Clever. Trust Mark to pre-book everything, yet present it as a spontaneous idea.

"Good job you didn't cancel everything, huh?" I ask, elbowing him gently in the ribs while we wait for the lift to come down.

He shrugs, giving me a sideways look.

"It was all non-refundable anyway, would've been a waste of time."

"Plus you could have always brought one of your other girlfriends…"

He grins for a split second, then leans over and gives me a peck on the cheek.

"Indeed, that's always an option."

The doors slide open in front of us and we step in.

There's a uniformed attendant, just like in the movies, who presses a button to take us all the way to the top. When we get there, an equally smartly dressed waiter shows us to our seats, right beside a large window. The view of the city down below is breathtaking.

"Wow," I say, unable to think of anything better.

"Yeah." Mark leans across the table, taking my hand. "Happy Valentine's day."

I respond with a smile, still speechless.

I would've never thought I'd be here with him, like this. With everything out in the open.

Ever since that night when the shit with Gareth happened, we've spent almost every spare moment together, getting to know each other. Although sometimes it's difficult not to panic and fear the worst, I can honestly say that I trust him now.

We've made a vow to not keep any more secrets.

And I fully intend to keep that promise.

★★★

AUTHOR'S NOTE

Firstly, thanks for reading *Sally*. It's a bit of a weird one, even for me, but I like to think that it's unusual in a good way.

The idea for this story came when while writing *The Rebound List,* which features a lot of the same characters (if you haven't read it yet, you may want to check it out). It wasn't relevant to the story at the time, but I couldn't help but wonder why Sally was so cynical about love. What had happened to her to make her so suspicious? Well, that question has now been answered.

Mark's reason for not settling down came up later, and it was a bit of a surprise to me at the time. But then, why not? It's a diverse world out there, and I like to think that the revelation that Marks enjoys dressing up as a woman at times works for his relationship with Sally on multiple levels.

I wanted to highlight that not every guy who cross-dresses is gay (actually, perhaps most of them are straight), and give both of them the chance to make it work despite everything. Mark gets to let go of the life of secrecy he had consigned himself to, and be accepted for who he is. And after finally getting closure on an event from her past which has had such a massive effect on who she is, Sally gets the chance to be in a relationship again. Not just that, her relationship with Mark is set to be just a bit more exciting than having only one person to be with forever. Plus, those who've read *The Rebound List*, already would've known that Sally does like to play with girls occasionally. It's a win-win.

When Sally and Mark first hook up, nobody could foresee just how far their relationship would go, least of all Sally herself. There were just so many things standing in the way, making a happy ending an unlikely outcome. That is why I've left the story at the point I did. For two characters with so much baggage, it wouldn't be likely that they'd get a happily ever after in what is essentially just a week. But worry not, I'd like to think they'll get there eventually.

I hope you, the reader, have enjoyed this story for what it is: the complicated coming together of people with secrets, who are finding a way of making it work against the odds.

If you got some pleasure out of it, feel free to connect or get in touch via email or social media; I do my best to answer every message I get as soon as possible!

x, Lorelei
- ❖ LMoone.com
- ❖ Lorelei Moone on Facebook

www.ingramcontent.com/pod-product-compliance
Lightning Source LLC
Chambersburg PA
CBHW070448170726
48291CB00005B/1653